In the Shadow of the Tower

Annette Vetter Adventure #5

December 1968

by Ann Carol Ulrich

"*I wonder what Terry's hiding,*" said Penny. "I mean ... this is really a mystery, Annette. He shows up in Ravensville, like a homeless person ... but he has a dad in Madison ... and he's carrying around the picture of this little girl. It gives me the creeps."

"Oh, Penny!" Annette scolded her friend. "I'm sure it's nothing like that. Terry seemed really nice."

"Well, you only saw him a couple of times. How do you know what he's like? He might be a thief or ... or a kidnapper."

"Your imagination is running wild again," Annette taunted.

But the situation had her worried. She prayed that Terry Knutson wasn't planning to rob the Randts.

What if he had conned his way into working for them, only to steal from them?

But that just didn't make sense.

To Sylvia

In the Shadow of the Tower

Ann Carol Ulrich

Earth Star Publications
Bayfield, Colorado

FIRST EDITION
First Printing November 2015

ISBN 978-0-944851-42-5

Printed in the United States of America

Cover photo courtesy of hdw.eweb4.com

Other Annette Vetter Books

The Mystery at Hickory Hill
Annette Vetter Adventure #1

The Secret of the Green Paint
Annette Vetter Adventure #2

The Pouting Pumpkin Mystery
Annette Vetter Adventure #3

The Legend of the Lantern
Annette Vetter Adventure #4

Other Young Adult Books

By Ann Carol Ulrich

The Root Cellar Mystery

Contents

In the Shadow of the Tower

1

Bus Stop

Bart watched the boy step off the bus at the end of the line. The other passengers had disembarked at earlier stops along the way.

It was almost midnight and frigid as he stood outside the depot. The station had closed an hour ago and Bart glimpsed the janitor still inside, finishing up.

He reached a fat hand up to his nose and stroked his bristly gray mustache. The older he got, the harder these late-night winter runs became. After a long day, Bart was looking forward to going home to his warm bed. He pulled his cap over his forehead as a gust of icy wind blew over him.

The boy looked over at him expectantly.

"Oh, you want to get your luggage." Bart reached into his pocket for the keys and opened the stow compartment on the side of the bus. Then he waited for the boy to collect his over-stuffed backpack.

"Been travelin' cross country, young fella?" asked the driver. Puffs of carbon dioxide rose from his mouth. "Well, I'll bet you're glad to finally get off this bus." He found his lighter and a pack of Marlboros in his jacket pocket.

With a quick swipe of his hand, the boy pushed some of

his long blond hair back over his ear and hoisted the navy blue backpack up over his narrow shoulders. The heavy green Air Force parka he wore, with its fur collar, helped cushion him from the punishing straps. He managed a kind smile for the bus driver, then murmured, "Got a ways to go yet."

The driver looked around. "Anybody meetin' ya?" He didn't see any waiting cars in the lot.

The boy shrugged, still with a smile on his face. "Nah." He turned to walk away.

"It's kind of late," Bart called out. "Almost midnight."

The lights inside the bus depot began to wink out, one by one. The janitor was going home. The boy sighed. "I know." He walked toward the dark street. No cars were anywhere.

"Well, wait a minute," said the driver. "How much farther you got to go, young man?"

The boy stopped and turned around. "Ravensville."

"That's thirty-five miles from here." The driver gaped at him. "You're not goin' there tonight, are ya?"

"No, but I can get started."

Shaking his head slowly from side to side, Bart flicked on his lighter, then ignited the end of his cigarette. A cold wind from the north blew some snow piled in a drift at the curb. He watched in wonder as the tall, thin boy pulled up his hood, adjusted his backpack, and walked away into the darkness.

2

A War Protester

Annette glanced at the clock on the classroom wall and sighed. Five more minutes of Geometry, then the final bell would ring and she would escape from the boredom of math class. Just one more week of classes and then it would be Christmas Break. She scanned the doodles on her notebook as Mr. Raymond rambled on at the chalk board, demonstrating some problems. She couldn't concentrate.

Out of the corner of her eye, Annette caught the dark-haired boy seated off to her right staring in her direction. With a quick sweep of her eyes up front, to be sure the teacher wasn't looking, she turned and smiled at Pete Randt, who smiled back.

Annette's pen began filling in the big block letters on the lower left cover of her notebook where she had printed ...

PETE

She had embellished the letters with shadows, ink scratches and different colors, to emphasize the fact that this was the boy she cared about. Then, she quickly opened up the notebook as Mr. Raymond announced what their next assignment was going to be.

After the bell rang, kids sprang from their desks and

gathered up their books and belongings, talking and laughing. The hall began to fill with students through with school for the day … and with the *weekend* ahead!

"Hi, Annette." Pete sidled up to Annette and they walked out of the room together.

"Pete, how's your baby sister doing?" Annette asked. It had only been three weeks since Mrs. Randt had brought baby Laura home from the hospital.

"Aw, she's fine," said Pete. "She cries a lot, though."

Annette giggled. "I thought that's what babies are supposed to do."

Pete blushed as they walked in the direction of Annette's locker, which she shared with her best friend Penny. "Yeah, I know … but it's been causing sleep deprivation."

Penny Duncan was already at the locker. "Hi, Pete." Her green eyes twinkled and she grinned at the two of them. "Oh, Annette, I can't stay for the meeting. I have to be at rehearsal for the pageant."

"What pageant?" asked Pete.

Annette turned to him. "Penny's got a big part in the Christmas pageant. She's going to play the piano."

"Really? I didn't know you played the piano." Pete stood and studied Penny in admiration.

"Yup," said Penny, stepping aside so that Annette could get into their locker. She twirled a strand of her long dark hair around her little finger.

"Well, how come you're not in Band?" asked Pete.

"I dunno," she said with a smile.

"Do you ever play accompaniments for Solos and Ensembles?"

"Oh, she gets asked every spring," Annette replied. She reached into the locker to gather the books she would need for the weekend.

"Yes, I usually volunteer. Why? Are you going to play a

trombone solo?"

Pete fidgeted, suddenly embarrassed. "I didn't think I was that good ... I don't know yet."

"Oh, you should perform a solo for sure," Penny encouraged. "I'd be happy to play the piano for you."

Pete smiled shyly. "Yeah, well, I'll think about it. I've got a few months to decide."

"And we've got a lot of practicing to do for the pageant before next week." After Annette was through, Penny started grabbing the books she would need for the weekend. "Annette, be sure to tell Lisa I'm sorry I can't help."

"She'll understand."

"Bye, Annette." Penny grabbed her coat and, with her books and purse in her other arm, hurried away down the corridor. "I'll phone you tonight," she called back.

Turning his attention back to Annette, Pete cleared his throat, then looked down at his feet. "I ... I just wanted to know ... uh ..."

"Hey, Pete!" a male voice called out.

Annette looked up and saw a couple of sophomore boys passing them. She recognized one of them as Steve Newton, whom she knew Penny still admired. Pete grinned and waved, then focused his brown eyes on Annette once again.

Annette wondered if Pete was gathering up nerve to ask her out. The possibility made her pulse quicken. "Yes, Pete?" She blinked.

"Uh ..." He hesitated, then smiled at her. "I was just wondering how Alice is coming along."

Annette relaxed and nodded her head at the farm boy she liked. "Alice is doing fine," she said with a comforting smile for him. "She's dried up, of course."

Pete immediately blushed. "Of course. I meant ..."

"Well, Mr. Duncan said it would probably happen by Christmas."

"Oh, that's good." Pete sighed. "Just remember ... if you need any help with her ... with the calving, I mean ... I want to be available."

Annette knew that Pete Randt had some experience with calving. Her Holstein cow, Alice, was due to calve within the next week or two. Annette's cows had calved for the first time a year ago, but she didn't feel that confident about it. Penny's family owned the largest dairy farm in Ravensville. Penny's older brother, Tim, and their father, Ray Duncan, had overseen the heifers' first calves. Annette had practically grown up as part of the Duncan family. She had kind of hoped Tim would also volunteer to help her, since he had overseen calvings many times and seemed to know what he was doing.

"Did I hear you say you're staying for a meeting?" Pete asked.

Annette turned to straighten up her locker. "Yeah, Future Farmers."

"Oh. Then you're not riding the bus home?"

"Nope."

"Well, okay then." He paused, then said, "Well, I gotta catch the bus." Pete shot Annette one last bashful smile, then left.

"Bye, Pete." Distracted by him, Annette started to put on her coat, still caught up in Pete's admiration of her.

Ever since school had started in September, she had hoped Pete would ask her out. When he seemed to like her, but failed to take that step, she had almost given up on him. Then, his cousin, who was visiting the Randts in October, had stepped in and asked Annette to Ravensville's Homecoming. That's what it had taken for Pete to finally get up the nerve to talk to her.

Of course, Thanksgiving weekend had been the very best. Annette and Penny had volunteered to baby-sit at the Randts' house while Mrs. Randt was in the hospital having her ninth baby. Pete and his brother Mark, being the oldest ones, had to work in the barn while their father was at the hospital. It ended up that the girls stayed with the Randt children the entire weekend, which had given Annette and Pete a really good opportunity to get to know each other better—not to mention the mystery they had solved.

"What? Annette? Are you going home *now?*"

Snapping out of her reverie, Annette stared at the thin, brown-haired senior girl with glasses who had stopped at her locker. "Oh! Lisa …No, I'm not going home. I'm coming to the meeting." Annette immediately took off her coat. "What was I thinking?" She giggled.

Practical and forgiving, Lisa Kowalski, who was president of Future Farmers of America, smiled and patted Annette's shoulder. "No … do bring your coat and your homework. We have to get those packages mailed today."

"I know." Annette grabbed her books and purse, then slammed her locker door. She followed the older girl down the hall to the Home Economics room.

"You and I are the only ones. Everyone else had to be somewhere else," said Lisa, who took her leadership position in FFA at Ravensville High School very seriously. "I hope we can get everything to the post office in time."

"When does it close?" asked Annette.

"I think we need to get the packages there by four-thirty," said Lisa. "Mrs. Leland told me the mail truck comes at five o'clock."

Annette took in the sight of a couple of dozen medium-sized brown packages lined up on the counters in the Home Ec room. For the last several days, the club members—about six girls and two boys—had divided and packaged up hundreds of home-baked cookies, fudge and candy. They had baked some of the treats after school, here in the Home Ec room, under the supervision of their advisor, Mrs. Leland. Annette and Penny had baked some of the Christmas cookies and gingerbread men at home, in the Vetters' kitchen, when it looked like they were going to come up short before the deadline.

"Oh, look at all *this!*"

Annette and Lisa turned around to find Mr. Raymond, the math teacher, standing at the door to the classroom. He was eyeing all of the packages ready to ship out.

"It looks like St. Nicholas has arrived early."

"We're just getting ready to take them to the post office," said Lisa.

"Oh, really? Where are you sending them?" asked the teacher.

Annette explained. "The FFA decided to send Christmas care packages to the soldiers in Vietnam."

"We all made candy, fudge and baked the cookies," added Lisa. She pulled on her coat and wheeled a cart over so they could load it up with packages.

"What a fantastic idea," said the math teacher. "That's really a terrific gesture."

"Mrs. Leland got a list of addresses of some of the troops from people she knows," explained Lisa.

Annette helped put some of the boxes on the cart and Mr. Raymond came in to help. Then they carried everything out to the parking lot, where Lisa had her parents' car waiting. They thanked the teacher, then loaded all of the packages inside while Lisa started the engine to warm things up.

"It feels like it's going to get really cold tonight," said Lisa.

"I know," agreed Annette. "It seems winter came too early this year." She slid into the passenger seat of Lisa's car and slammed the door shut.

"It sure did. We had that huge blizzard at Thanksgiving."

Annette recalled how the snow storm had come the night of Thanksgiving, when she and Penny had been at the Randts' with the children. The blizzard had made travel conditions dangerous so that Grandma Dawson had been unable to travel, which meant Annette and Penny stayed at the Randts' and baby-sat through Monday, when school had been called off.

The snow had stayed. Even though it was just mid-December, Annette was already tired of the Wisconsin cold and the snow.

"Are you doing anything special this year over the holidays?" Lisa asked as she put the car into reverse.

Annette sighed. "Not really." Then she shot a smile at the older girl. "Well, my mom wanted us to drive up to Minocqua. I've got an aunt and uncle there who have a cottage on the lake."

"Cool," said Lisa.

"But she can't take the time off of work."

"Oh, too bad."

"Yeah, it is." Annette stared into her lap, recalling how her mother had wanted so much to get away. Mrs. Vetter, who worked as a nurse at Ravensville General Hospital, didn't get much time off. She worked the night shift most of the week. Tomorrow was Saturday, and she had the day off for once.

"We're going to have a houseful over Christmas," said Lisa. As she pulled out of the school parking lot, she chattered on about her cousins who were planning to visit from Minnesota. "It's going to be a zoo!" She caught Annette's surprised reaction, then added, "Well, there are five kids in our family as it is, and that means a lot of us will have to sleep in the basement. Thank goodness we have two bathrooms, at least."

"Yeah, so do we," muttered Annette. Then she felt a twinge of self-pity, something she had been experiencing too much lately. Two bathrooms in the Vetter farmhouse and only two people living under the one roof.

They drove three blocks into the downtown area of

Ravensville and found that the post office parking area was filled with cars. Annette could see people carrying packages into the post office.

"Oh no, where am I going to park?" Lisa began to fret. She passed the post office, then turned left onto a side road. "Oh dear ... and we have all these boxes to carry in."

"It will be okay," said Annette. She began looking for a place for Lisa to park. "There's one over there."

"Where?"

Annette pointed.

Lisa frowned. "That's too far away." She circled the block and slowly pulled into the post office parking lot just as a Volkswagen bus was pulling out of one of the stalls. "Oh, good," said Lisa.

After they parked and Lisa turned off the engine, Annette got out of the car and started grabbing a few packages off the back seat. The wind had picked up and whipped the scarf across her cheeks. She reached her free hand up and swept the scarf aside.

Just as she did, she saw a tall boy in a heavy green parka heading toward the doors of the post office. Dressed in ragged blue jeans, he was tall with long blond hair and whiskers. Their eyes met for a second, and then he adjusted a heavy navy blue backpack and went inside the building.

"Don't take too much at one time," said Lisa, bending over on the other side of the car. "We can come back a few more times, if we have to."

"I wish some of the others in FFA could have helped out," said Annette. "Penny's the only one who would have stayed if she hadn't needed to go to practice. Where were the others?"

"Yeah, I know." Lisa struggled to balance three boxes and kicked the door shut on her side with her boot. "My brother Scott is in the pageant too. He sings in the choir."

The girls carried their boxes up to the building and stood

for a few seconds, trying to figure out how one of them was going to open the door. A man was coming out and held the door open for them.

"Thanks," said Lisa. They carried the boxes into the lobby, which was small but crowded with about ten people waiting in line. There was only one postal clerk station open.

"Good grief, this is going to take all evening," Lisa grumbled.

"Maybe they'll let us put them on the end of that counter," suggested Annette, indicating a section that was almost bare.

Lisa led the way over and they unloaded their packages. "Is this okay? We've got more," she called to the postal clerk, who was busy and merely nodded at them as she weighed some packages for an elderly lady.

Annette noticed the young man in the green parka with the backpack was at the counter, filling out some kind of card. He had his back toward them as they headed out to the car to bring in another load of packages bound for overseas.

After they brought in the third load of boxes, there was hardly any room left on the end of the counter. "How many more?" the clerk called out to them. She didn't appear to be pleased at the sight of so many packages going into the mail.

Lisa looked down and tapped her forehead, then said to the postal clerk, "About seven more."

Somebody in line groaned and another person chuckled in response.

When Annette followed Lisa into the post office with the last load, which they held rather than place on the counter— since there was no more room—Annette saw the blond guy in the parka standing ahead of them as they got in line. There were still two people ahead of him.

"Gad, I hope these get there in time for Christmas," said Lisa.

"We probably should have had them mailed out last

week," said Annette, "but I don't see how we could have."

"Well, baking all those goodies took forever," added Lisa.

"Yeah, but even if they don't get there for Christmas Day, the troops will have them for New Year's." Annette shifted the weight for comfort.

"Oh *my*," said a woman standing in line ahead of the boy in the green parka. She turned to the girls and smiled broadly. "Are all of those boxes for our troops?"

Lisa grinned. "They are."

"Where are they going?" someone else asked.

Annette turned and saw a heavyset older girl in a hippie dress standing behind them in line. The girl's coat was open, showing a set of wooden love beads hanging from her neck. She had long, frizzy red hair, and rosy cheeks from being out in the cold air. "They're going to the soldiers in Vietnam," Annette told her.

Immediately, the heavyset girl rolled her eyes and mumbled something under her breath.

The lady who had spoken up first caught the reaction and confronted the girl. "Do you have a problem with that, miss?"

"*Next*, please."

The lady swiveled around and gave her full attention to the postal clerk while the boy in the green parka glanced back at Annette, then took a few steps ahead in line. Annette and Lisa followed suit, but the hippie girl behind them was not through.

"The war in Vietnam is illegal and immoral," she stated in a loud voice.

Both Annette and Lisa turned around to face her. Annette could see that Lisa was embarrassed and turned away. She hadn't expected the FFA president, of all people, to act cowardly when confronted by a hippie who opposed the Vietnam war.

"Look," said Annette, who, even though she was just a

sophomore, wasn't afraid to speak her mind. "We're just sending some cookies and fudge for Christmas. It's for the soldiers ..."

"I don't care what's in those stupid packages," cried the girl. "You are supporting the *war!* That makes you *war-mongers.*"

"What?" Annette scrunched up her face. "I don't know what you're talking about. We are not ..."

"You should be ashamed," the girl continued. "How can you support something that gets people killed? Hey, what business does the US have going over there in the first place?"

Flabbergasted, Annette glanced around. She could see that the lady ahead of the boy in the green parka was finishing up her business with the postal clerk. She wished they could just leave, but they had to finish mailing all those boxes. The hippie continued to voice her opposition to the Vietnam conflict.

"Just ignore her, Annette," whispered Lisa, who was trembling.

"I heard that," the hippie girl snapped. "How many more are going to die? When are they ever going to learn that bombs and fighting are not the answer? I hate America for what it's doing."

Some people who had gotten in line behind the hippie girl had disturbed looks on their faces and some pretended to be busy or not paying attention to the altercation.

Annette's pulse was racing. She didn't want to feed the fury. She was almost afraid this heavyset girl could get physically aggressive.

Then the tall boy ahead of them turned around and stared right into the hippie girl's face. "What is it you want?" he asked in a calm, but authoritative voice.

The hippie girl's eyes widened and she opened her mouth to reply to him, but just then it was his turn at the counter.

"*Next!*" shouted the postal clerk.

Annette whispered something into Lisa's ear and Lisa nodded. Annette said to the heavyset girl, "You can go next. We have a lot of packages to mail. Please ... we want you to go ahead of us."

Defeated, the heavyset girl pouted and mumbled, "That's more like it."

Annette and Lisa exchanged glances. Then Annette heard the boy at the counter ask the clerk a question in a quiet voice. She hadn't been able to make out what he had said.

"General delivery?" the clerk replied. She looked at the form he had filled out. "We don't have anything here for you, Terry. Besides, you didn't fill out the other side of the form. And you'll have to show me some form of I.D." She handed the card back to him, then gave him a pen and directed him over to the counter where the girls had placed their packages. He moved over, but Annette noticed he couldn't find any space in which to write.

"Oh, let me move some of these," said Annette. She grabbed about four of the packages as Lisa stepped aside to let the hippie girl take her turn ahead of them.

The boy named Terry rewarded Annette with a warm smile and blue eyes that penetrated hers with a gentleness that seemed unusual. "Very kind ... thank you," he said, then began to write on the form.

Annette and Lisa, along with all the other customers in line at the post office, put up with the hippie girl's incessant complaints as she demanded a new post office key because hers was lost, and she thought it was *unconstitutional* that she had to pay a dollar for a new key.

"What does *she* know about the Constitution?" Lisa whispered to Annette, and they both giggled.

Finally, it was their turn. The postal clerk, looking bedraggled after a long day waiting on customers with holiday packages, did her best to get through the twenty-five boxes. Annette tried not to let it bother her that people were lined up behind her to the door of the post office. She glanced at the clock and thought it was a good thing they had at least made the package deadline.

By the time they were done, some of the post office customers had left to come back the next morning. Annette followed Lisa out the door to the car. She noticed that Terry, the boy in the green parka, had already left too.

"I'll drop you off at the school," said Lisa as she pulled out of the parking space. "Are you gonna wait for Penny?"

"Well, I think she's gonna be at least an hour," said Annette. "I have to get home to do my chores."

Lisa laughed. "Yeah, me too. I'll just drive you home then." Lisa lived in the country, but on the other side of Ravensville from Annette and Penny. "Boy, I'm sure glad we got that project out the door."

"You can say that again," said Annette.

When Lisa dropped her off at the end of the Vetter driveway on Ogden Road, the sun had disappeared behind the woods in back of the farmhouse. Ginger, who had been waiting on the porch for her since her mother had left for work earlier in the day, perked up his collie ears and ran to meet her as Lisa backed out and drove away.

"Ginger!" Annette knelt down and rubbed the red collie's white mane as he whined, his tail swishing, and licked her face. She stood up and looked over at the chicken yard, where the hens were slowly making their way into the hen house for the night. The snow was trampled by their feet in the poultry yard and a hen cackled inside as Annette made her way to the house to change out of her dress.

Fifteen minutes later, she was back outside in her heavy coat, jeans and boots, where she made her way to the barn, accompanied by Ginger. A cold wind blew from the north and the woods looked stark and barren without the leaves. It had snowed twice since Thanksgiving, so the ground had a good cover of insulation. Annette sighed, thinking it was going to be a very long time before spring came and she could smell green grass and see buds on all those beautiful trees she loved so much.

Inside the barn, she collected the pail and a rag, then went to milk Elizabeth, the Holstein that was still giving milk. Alice, nine months pregnant, stood in her stall, swollen in the belly and with such a tired look in her brown bovine eyes. Annette went over and stroked Alice's head gently, crooning to her that everything was going to be fine and that it wouldn't be much longer.

Elizabeth mooed loudly as if to remind Annette that she needed to be milked — and *now*. As Annette pulled the milking stool up and sat to begin the chore, her mind went over the events of the last few weeks. She did most of her serious thinking and planning during the morning and evening milking sessions. Ginger lay down in the hay and watched her, his long nose cushioned between his white front paws.

After the excitement that had occurred on the Randts' property after Thanksgiving, life had gone back to normal, for the most part. The deer poachers had been caught, although it had been unfortunate that one of them had been shot dead by the game warden. At least she and Penny hadn't frozen to death in the underground bunker the poachers had thrown them into, or *worse* — had Pete Randt not come to the rescue, along with Penny's brother Tim and the man, Earl Warner.

Reid Anderson, who might have left the girls to the fate of the killers, redeemed himself when he helped in their rescue, and was allowed to stay and continue working for the Randts' as their farm hand. Penny had a crush on Reid, but after a couple of weeks, he left the area. Annette was glad that Penny didn't flip out after that. The attraction had worn off somewhat after their adventure. Penny still had her eye on Steve Newton, a popular boy in their grade at Ravensville High.

As for Earl Warner, the land developer who had wanted to buy out Mr. Randt, he also left the area, defeated from his purpose. Annette cringed to think that Earl had almost talked Mrs. Vetter into marrying him. He would have made her sell their forty acres, and then she and her mother would have gone to live in Black River Falls to start a new life.

"I didn't want to start a new life," Annette mumbled out loud as she pulled on Elizabeth's teats, squirting gushes of white milk that rang against the steel bottom of the pail. She saw Ginger's ears perk at the sound of her voice and smiled at her dog. "Oh, Ginger, I couldn't go live in the city. This is my home ... *here* ... with you and Mom and ... and ... Elizabeth and Alice and the chickens ..."

Suddenly, Annette gasped as a sob broke loose. She let the tears flow. There was nobody around to see her, after all. Since Ginger was a good listener, she unloaded on him.

"It's just ... it's just that ..." She sniffed and wiped the back of her hand over the end of her wet nose. "Oh ... why do I feel so alone? Mom's at work most of the time. The house isn't that big, but when I'm alone, it feels so ... so ... *empty!*" She sobbed again.

Annette had been raised an only child. She had lost her father when she was only 4, and her mother had never considered remarrying until last month, when Earl Warner, whom she had met at the hospital, had started courting her and had proposed to her. But when Mrs. Vetter found out that Earl Warner just wanted to grab a lot of the farm land in Ravensville for a big, profitable housing development, that was the end of it.

"I know it broke her heart, Ginger." Annette sniffed. "Poor Mom. But it was for the best, really it was. Mr. Warner was taking advantage of her." It made her angry to think of that aspect. "Mom always told me she couldn't love anyone except Dad." Yet, somehow, Annette believed her mom had actually fallen in love with Earl.

Mr. Vetter had died from an illness in the prime of his life. She barely remembered her dad, but he had been gentle, kind and had worked as a park ranger in Black River Falls, and then had purchased the forty-acre little farm with its surrounding woods that Annette loved with all her heart.

During her childhood, while her mother worked, Annette had spent most of her time at the Duncan farm down the road, where she had practically become a part of the family with Penny and her older brother Tim for company.

But in the last two or three weeks, Annette had noticed how sullen her mother had grown. The usually cheery Mrs. Vetter had grown quiet and seemed to be wallowing in despair. When they had planned on taking the trip to Minocqua for Christmas, Annette had been excited. But then Mrs. Vetter said she couldn't get the time off. They would have to stay in Ravensville.

"Some Christmas it's going to be," murmured Annette. "Mom working all the time … all this snow and cold … and not to mention Alice." She glanced up at her pregnant cow. "Oh, Alice, I'm sorry, I didn't mean it that way, girl." With the calf expected to be born close to Christmas Day, Annette knew it was best for them to stay home. She definitely *did* want to be there when Alice had her calf.

Besides, Pete Randt had said he wanted to help with the calving—Pete, whom she liked so much and had gotten to know a lot better since Thanksgiving. Pete was still shy, though. He hadn't asked her out since she had gone to the Homecoming dance with him and his cousin Luke. She smiled, remembering how unusual it had been to go to the big dance with *two* dates instead of one. She had hoped that Pete would start dating her, but she knew he didn't have a car, and he didn't have any money. Dating was kind of out of the question … for now.

Still, she longed for someone to spend time with. "If only I had a brother or a sister, like Penny," Annette said to herself.

"Annette, you've got to be crazy," Penny had told her time and again. "Believe me, sisters and brothers are overrated."

Annette didn't believe that. Sure, you argue sometimes, you get sick of them being around … or at least that was what she had been told … but it sure seemed better than being an only child.

Finishing up the milking, Annette fed the cows, filled the water trough, then stored the milk. Then she and Ginger went to close up the chickens and collect eggs. Dusk was spreading over the sky. She sighed as she trudged with her egg basket, her collie at her side, toward the dark farmhouse.

3

Annette's Christmas List

"Rehearsal was a riot," exclaimed Penny later that evening, when she telephoned Annette. "I wish you could have been there. I'm starting to sound a little better, finally. At least I only made a few mistakes with the music. Kathy and Debbie are in the choir. Hey, did you and Lisa get those packages mailed?"

"We did." Annette then told her friend about the heavy-set hippie girl who had taunted them at the post office about sending Christmas packages to the soldiers in Vietnam.

"How rude!" Penny cried, infuriated. "I can't believe it. The nerve!"

"What are you doing tomorrow?" Annette asked.

Penny sighed. "Mom wants me to baby-sit. She and Dad want to go Christmas shopping."

"Oh." Annette wasn't sure she wanted to be part of baby-sitting Penny's younger sister, Karen. Usually she didn't mind.

"Karen wants to make Christmas cookies," said Penny. "I'm so sick of baking cookies."

Annette was too. "Mom's gonna be home tomorrow. She might want to do something. We don't see each other much lately."

"Oh, I understand," said Penny cheerfully. "Hey, did you write your Christmas list yet?"

"Kind of," said Annette. Her list was on the dining room table, unfinished. Their English teacher had made a class assignment out of writing a holiday wish list.

"Well, I'm working on mine," said Penny.

"Actually, I promised Mom I'd help her address Christmas cards. Otherwise I'd come over and help with Karen and the cookies."

"Annette, you don't have to make up any excuses." Penny giggled. "I'll talk to ya later. Tim is calling me."

"Okay. Bye, Pen." Annette hung up the phone. Then she fingered the sheet of paper on the table in front of her — the Christmas list she had started earlier. She picked it up and read it:

MY CHRISTMAS LIST

Albums
> **The Cream (must include "Sunshine of Your Love")**
> **Steppenwulf and Tommy James and The Shondelles**

Oil Paint Set
> **(Maybe some canvas paper to practice on)**

Nylons (Plain, but also colored and textured, Size 9-1/2)

Flashlight (Small, but not a pen light ... please!)

False Eyelashes (Not to wear, really — just to have fun with)

Pullover tops (to go with my brown Levis, size 34)

Stationery (psychedelic paper, but not too flowery)

A Horse

Annette picked up her pen and scribbled one more item on her Wish List ...

A Boy (16 or older, and taller, with a nice crop of hair)

Then she made a face and thought about scratching that last item off her list. But before she could do that, there was a knock on the back door. Ginger jumped up from where he was resting under the table and barked as he followed her into the kitchen to see who was there. She flicked on the porch light.

A medium-sized man wearing a brown leather coat and ear muffs smiled at her when she opened the door. "Hello, Annette."

"Doctor Slater!" Annette stepped back and invited him inside, but he stayed on the porch.

"I was just down at the Duncan farm," explained the veterinarian. "One of Ray's bulls needed a treatment. Tim mentioned one of your cows is ready to give birth. Is that right?"

"Why, yes."

"Tim asked me to stop over and have a quick look. You know, just to make sure she's doing okay."

Annette grabbed her farm coat off the hook behind the door, then stepped outside with Ginger brushing past. His tail wagged as he greeted the veterinarian. Then she led him to the barn. He had a flashlight with him as they made their way down the snowy path.

Inside, Annette switched on the lights to reveal both her Holsteins standing quietly in their stalls. *How nice of Tim to ask for Doc Slater to check on Alice,* she thought. She watched as the vet examined Alice, who lowed softly as he palpated her and checked her vital signs.

"Sounds good," said Doc Slater as he removed his rubber gloves and threw them into a bag in his briefcase.

"Is she close?" asked Annette.

"I'd say ... another week, at least."

Annette put her hand on Alice's neck.

"The other cow ... when's she due again?" asked Doc.

Elizabeth turned her head and gazed at them, as if she

knew he had asked about her.

"Let's see." Annette scratched her head, gazing at Elizabeth's slightly bulging flanks. "Mr. Duncan artificially inseminated her last August."

"Oh, well, she's got a while yet. Spring ... probably sometime in May."

Annette followed Doc Slater out of the barn and Ginger tagged along. She switched off the lights, then closed the barn door. "Thanks for coming out," she said.

"No problem," said Doc Slater. "I was in the neighborhood." He started walking to his truck. "Call me if you have any problems."

After he left, Annette went inside to wash up. She found some left-over peanut butter fudge in the refrigerator and nibbled on it while she watched some TV. When it got to be 10 o'clock, she could barely keep her eyes open and decided to go upstairs to bed.

She was already asleep when Mrs. Vetter's car turned into the driveway an hour later.

The next morning, Annette was up at her usual time to milk the cows and open up the chicken coop. Her mother was still sleeping when she came back into the house after doing chores. She noticed that her Christmas Wish List had been moved from the dining room table and was stuck to the front of the refrigerator door with a magnet. Her mother had obviously found it and read it. Annette smiled to think that she had left that last "wish" on the list.

"Good morning, dear," said Mrs. Vetter an hour later. Annette had curled up on the living room couch for a morning snooze, but sat up at the sound of her mother's voice.

"Oh hi, Mom." Annette sat up and stretched.

"Have you had breakfast yet?" asked her mother.

"No." Annette yawned and went into the kitchen.

"I'll fix us something." Mrs. Vetter very slowly pulled a coffee cup out of the cupboard and filled it with black coffee from the electric percolator on the counter. Annette had made a small pot earlier, just for the benefit of her mother. She rarely drank coffee herself—only when she really needed to stay awake for something.

"What are you and Penny up to this weekend?"

Annette found a glass, then opened the refrigerator to get out the orange juice. "Nothing." Annette explained how Penny had to baby-sit.

Mrs. Vetter, still dressed in her robe and slippers, sat down at the kitchen table. She held her head and sighed.

"What's wrong, Mom? Do you have a headache?"

The small woman whose reddish-brown hair was just a shade lighter than Annette's, only cut short and styled differently, looked at her daughter with heavy eyelids. "No, it's just ... kind of rough right now."

"Did you have a hard night at work?" Annette sipped her orange juice.

Mrs. Vetter slowly brought the coffee cup to her lips. "No ... everything's okay."

Annette waited for more of an explanation, but Mrs. Vetter was silent. After a minute, Annette put down her juice glass and leaned over. "Mom. Please tell me what's wrong."

"Nothing is wrong." The woman took another sip of her coffee as she stared straight ahead.

"But, Mom, you've been so down lately." Annette decided not to hide the fact that she had noticed more than a few times that her mother seemed depressed. "You're always so ... quiet."

Mrs. Vetter faked a smile, but it wasn't convincing. "Annette, I'm okay. Really."

"Well, do you wanna talk about it?" prompted Annette.

Silence. Mrs. Vetter sat and stared into her coffee cup. She offered no words.

Finally, Annette stood up. "Okay. I'll make us some pancakes. Do you want blueberries?"

"Sure."

Annette went to the pantry to retrieve flour, baking soda, salt and a mixing bowl. She had a feeling she knew what her mother's problem was. It was the same thing *she* had been feeling lately ... loneliness. With winter setting in, the long dark days, the empty house ... both of them were *lonely*.

Annette began to feel uneasy. Hadn't she been the one who had convinced her mother not to marry Earl Warner? What would have happened if she had not had a fit about it, and exposed the man's conniving schemes to rob people out of their farm land? He hadn't really done anything illegal, it was just the way he went about it that didn't seem right. Yet her mother had been smitten by the man ... and apparently he was wealthy and willing to make them his family. He had even offered to send Annette to college.

"Still, I couldn't bear it if we'd had to move away," Annette muttered to herself as she mixed the milk and eggs and vanilla with the dry ingredients in a bowl. Her mother had gone upstairs to get dressed. The thought of giving up their forty acres and the only life she had ever known, to go live in the city ... was just unthinkable.

Ginger watched from his post underneath the kitchen table, hanging on every word. She tried to rationalize the whole thing. "Yet ... maybe Mom needs someone. Maybe she still loves him ... maybe I stuck my nose into something I shouldn't have." She kept her mouth shut when she heard Mrs. Vetter's footsteps coming down the stairs.

Her mother emerged, dressed in blue slacks and a white sweater. She had combed her hair and put on fresh lipstick. "Mmm, smells good," said Mrs. Vetter.

Annette turned on the griddle on top of the stove, then

winked at Ginger. "I'm just starting to heat up the pan. Are you feeling better, Mom?"

Mrs. Vetter gave her daughter a quick hug. "Yes, darling. Thanks."

Annette sighed with relief.

4

Job Inquiry

Mr. Brown was stocking the shelves in the small clothing section of his country store when the bell on the front door tinkled. He slid another pair of new snow boots onto the bottom shelf, making sure that the pricetag showed. Then he glanced up to watch as a tall, attractive young man with blond hair and whiskers walked in from the cold. The boy looked to be about 16 or 17 and wore a heavy green Air Force parka. Strapped to his back was a large navy pack.

"Good morning," the teen-ager called to Mr. Brown.

The storekeeper stood up straight and smiled cordially. "Good morning yourself. How can I help you, young man?"

The boy looked around at everything in the store, then walked over with his hands in his pockets. "I was wondering if you might need any help."

Surprised, Mr. Brown studied the tall, slender figure. The kind blue eyes seemed to give off warmth along with the smile. Yet he was cautious. This young man was a stranger to him— and he had long hair and was trying to grow a beard. "What's your name, young man?"

The boy pulled the black stocking cap off his head to reveal a heavy crop of whitish-blond hair and bangs that

27

covered very light eyebrows. "Terry Knutson," he said. "I'm in need of a job."

"I see," said Mr. Brown. He walked over to the counter to stand behind the cash register. "Well, I really don't need to hire any help in the store right now."

Terry turned to head out the door, his head bowed. Then he stopped and appealed to the storekeeper once more. "I don't need to work *in* the store," he said. "I can cut wood or shovel snow. I can even clean up."

Mr. Brown rubbed his chin and thought a moment. "Where are you from?"

"Uh … nowhere really." Terry wouldn't look the storekeeper in the eye.

"Where are you staying?"

Terry looked up briefly and shrugged. "I just got into town, actually."

"Don't you know anybody here?" asked Mr. Brown.

With a sniff, Terry shook his head, then again turned to leave.

"Wait," said Mr. Brown. "I'm sure somebody around these parts has some work for you to do. Why don't you come back tomorrow? I'll kind of … put the word out." He winked.

Terry smiled at Mr. Brown. "I appreciate that, sir."

"There's no phone number I can reach you at?"

Terry shook his head.

"You don't have any place to stay?"

"No."

Mr. Brown rubbed his chin again and rolled his eyes a bit. Finally, he said, "You look like a decent sort. I know a fella on Gaston Road who could use some farm help. You know anything about cows?"

Terry swallowed, then stared down at his feet. "Not really."

"I take it then that you didn't grow up in the country."

"No, sir. My dad was in the military."

"Oh, is that so?" Mr. Brown's eyebrows shot up.

"We moved around a lot," explained Terry. "But I was actually born in Madison."

"Well, don't you have any relatives?"

Terry was silent a moment, then shot Mr. Brown a quick smile as he headed for the door. "Not really. At least none that I know of."

"Check back with me," called Mr. Brown.

The door tinkled as the boy left the store. Mr. Brown went back to his stocking chore and muttered to himself, "Vagabonds ... it doesn't matter what time of year ..."

That afternoon, Annette helped her mother address and sign Christmas cards. They turned on the television and watched *A Miracle on 34th Street,* starring Natalie Wood. Mrs. Vetter cried at the end, which worried Annette a little as she scribbled their return address on the upper left hand corner of each envelope. She wished her mom was not so sad.

Before supper Annette went out and did her farm chores, then read her book up in her room while Mrs. Vetter made a simple supper. The telephone rang downstairs, and a moment later Mrs. Vetter called up the stairway. "Annette, Penny's on the phone."

"Okay, Mom." Annette stuck the bookmark—an old Nestlés Crunch bar wrapper—in the book, then hurried downstairs to answer the phone in the dining room. In the kitchen she passed her mom, frying a couple of pork chops on the stove.

"Hi, Pen," Annette said into the mouthpiece.

"I thought Mom and Dad would never get home," Penny chattered. "You're lucky you didn't come over here to help me baby-sit Karen."

"Why?"

Penny sighed. "The little squirt wasn't feeling well. We

started making Christmas cookies, but she whined and cried and said she didn't want to finish frosting them, after all that rolling out the dough, cutting out the cookies and baking them."

"Oh no, is she sick?"

"I don't think so, Annette, but she's got a sore throat. Mom made her go to bed."

"It's that darn time of year."

"I know." Penny sighed. "Hey, wanna do something tomorrow?"

"You don't have to rehearse?"

"Not until Monday," said Penny. "We can go sledding on our hill, or skating at the pond."

"Anything sounds great," said Annette. "I've been cooped up inside all day."

"And maybe we can take a walk down the road," suggested Penny. "I've got some baby-sitting money. Maybe I'll buy you some gum at Brown's Store."

Annette made a sound of disgust. "I hate gum, Pen."

"Okay then ... a chocolate bar."

"What time?"

"After church ... I'll be over as soon as we get home."

After Annette hung up, she helped her mother set the table in the kitchen, and then they sat down and had their supper of pork chops, apple sauce and canned peas from last summer's vegetable garden. Annette poured herself and her mother a large glass of fresh cow's milk.

"If you go sledding tomorrow, dress warmly," said Mrs. Vetter.

Annette smiled. It was a relief to have her mother acting a little more normal.

The sun came out on Sunday. At noon, Annette and Penny, dressed in coats, scarves and mittens, started down Ogden

Road on foot. They left the Duncans' mailbox at the end of the long driveway and headed for Browns' Store, which was a mile and a half away. Both Ginger and Penny's sheepdog, The Cheeze, accompanied them as they usually did when they hiked to the country store on the corner of the highway.

"What's Tim up to these days?" Annette asked casually.

"Busy," said Penny. "He and Dad are always out in the barn. Tim's been griping because he can't go out as much, but I think he's glad to get the extra money."

"Think he'll leave for college next year?" asked Annette. Penny's brother was in his final year of high school and had mentioned on occasion that he might go to college at Eau Claire.

"I don't think he's put in his application yet," said Penny. "At least *we* don't have to worry about that for two more years." She laughed. "I don't even know what I want to be."

"Me neither," admitted Annette. She didn't even want to think about what her life might be like after high school. Some of their friends at school just couldn't seem to wait until graduating, but Annette wanted this phase of her life to continue for as long as it could. Of course, it would be a lot more fun when she was a little older and was having dates … preferably with Pete Randt.

As if reading her mind—which she often seemed to do— Penny asked, "Have you talked to Pete at all this weekend?"

"Why, no," said Annette. "Not since we saw him Friday after school."

Penny winced. "I'm sure they're busy over at the Randts' farm, especially since Reid left."

"Yeah," said Annette. "I'm sure they could use some extra help … if they could even afford to pay someone."

"Reid thought he could work for nothing after what happened," Penny rambled. "He told me room and board was good enough. But I guess he got a better offer."

"Are you sorry he left?"

"Oh, not really," said Penny. "He was too broke to take me out."

"That's Pete's problem, too." Annette sighed. "But just think ... in a year, we'll be juniors, and a lot of guys in our class will have their driver's licenses. That should make a big difference."

"Or not," pouted Penny. "Steve Newton is so stuck up, I'm sure he'll never ask any girl out."

"You need to get over him," said Annette.

"I'm working on it," Penny said mysteriously.

Half an hour later, they arrived at Browns' Store, cold and eager to get inside, where it was warm. The dogs remained outside by the door. There was a car and a blue Willys Jeep parked in the lot. Mr. Brown was ringing up some beer and snacks for a man at the counter. Annette followed Penny over to the candy shelves and they began searching for their favorite treats.

Annette was aware of someone going into the restroom at the back of the store. "I need to visit the little girl's room before we walk back home," she told Penny. Then she picked out a Snickers bar and handed it to Penny. "Are we getting anything today for your mom?"

"Oh yeah," said Penny. "She needs food coloring, if Mr. Brown has any."

"More Christmas cookies?"

"Actually, she just needs to replace what Karen used," explained Penny. "That little brat decided to paint some pictures up in her room with Mom's food colors ... and she spilled them on the sheets and blankets. Mom was livid!"

Annette giggled. "At least your little sister is imaginative. Is she feeling better today?"

"Her sore throat went away, if that's what you mean. She's still acting real bratty. Why do little kids get that way just before Christmas?"

Penny looked around on the shelves by the baking ingredients and finally found a small box of food coloring. They took it and the candy up to the cash register, and Mr. Brown rang up the prices.

"Your dad needing any extra help on the farm?" Mr. Brown asked Penny.

"Well, they always can use help," she replied. "But they're getting along okay, I guess. Why?"

Mr. Brown said, "A young man came in here yesterday asking for work. Seemed to be a bit down and out, if you know what I mean."

"I don't think my dad wants any more like that," said Penny.

"You mean after Dave Beck?" Annette smirked. Dave Beck had worked as a ranch hand at the Duncan farm in October, but had turned out to be a drug smuggler. She would never forget how he had caught Penny and herself in the back of his camper that was parked illegally in the Vetters' woods. They had discovered crates of drugs when he had been away from his truck. Pete, his cousin Luke Elliott, and Tim had come to the girls' rescue just in the nick of time. Annette sighed at the memory.

"I'm sure he's right about that," said Mr. Brown. "Well, if you hear of anyone ..."

Annette wandered over toward the restroom while Penny paid for the items. A few moments later, the door opened and out stepped its occupant. Annette gasped in surprise as she stared into the face of the hippie girl who had been so outspoken at the post office on Friday. The red-haired young woman had bell bottoms on and smelled of cigarette smoke.

The girl recognized her and stared back. "Oh, it's *you*." Annette stepped aside to let the girl pass, but the hippie placed her hands on her fat hips. "You're the patriotic little warmonger that was in line at the post office. Well, don't be surprised if all your efforts end up as *crumbs* by the time they get to Indochina."

Both Mr. Brown and Penny had stopped what they were doing and gazed over at the hippie girl and Annette. Befuddled and feeling humiliated to confront this rude person again, Annette dodged her and ran into the restroom. She closed the door quickly and locked it.

When Annette came out, she met Penny's curious stare. Mr. Brown had resumed whatever he had been doing, and there was no sign of the hippie woman. No one else was in the store. "What was that all about?" asked Penny as they led the dogs back to the road.

Annette explained on the walk home, which led to a long discussion about hippies. Ravensville was small enough and rural enough that the culture had not gripped it, but they knew about the protests at the universities around the state, and in particular the violence that had erupted on Madison's campus.

"See you in the morning," Penny called as Annette and her collie left Penny and her sheepdog at the end of the Duncans' driveway. It was only mid-afternoon, but the long shadows from the setting sun made the woods on both sides close in around them.

Annette thought more about hippies as she walked the last quarter mile to the Vetters' driveway. She hoped seeing that rude girl in the store was the last time they would meet. As she approached the house, her mother came out of the farm house, dressed in her coat with her nurse's uniform underneath.

"You mean it's already time for you to go to work, Mom?"

Mrs. Vetter smiled. "Don't stay up too late, dear."

"I won't, Mom."

"And do your homework."

"Don't worry."

Mrs. Vetter climbed into the car, started up the engine, then left for town. Annette stood in the silence, then looked toward the empty house and suddenly felt very alone.

5

A Wisp of Smoke

Monday morning there was a coating of fresh snow on the ground as Annette went out to the barn to milk the cow before breakfast. Daybreak showed a rosy glow to the east, masked by the naked trees across Ogden Road.

She finished her chores and fixed herself a bowl of oatmeal and some toast. At seven-fifteen Penny came by, bundled up in her winter jacket and her boots with the pointy toes.

"It's so cold!" Annette let Ginger out onto the enclosed porch, where he lay down on his rug with his white paws between his long snout. The collie knew Annette was going to school and he couldn't follow her.

Annette was dressed in her warmest coat with a long scarf that her mother had knitted wrapped around her neck and head. Her legs were exposed to the bitter Wisconsin cold with just nylons underneath a skirt that hung a couple of inches above her knees. No girls she knew wore pants to school—they braved the cold rather than be labeled "odd."

She pulled on the boots that fit over her loafers, grabbed her books and purse, then walked with Penny through the fresh layer of white powder in the driveway. Mrs. Vetter's car had gotten a dusting, but there wasn't time to clean the snow off for her mother.

The bus stop was at the corner of Ogden Road and Tower Drive, about one-third of a mile from Annette's farm. The girls usually rode the rural school bus, although on days that they were late, Tim would grudgingly give them a ride. Annette preferred the bus these days because Pete was on it.

"I need to tell Tim thank you for having Dick Slater come over last night," Annette told her best friend. "He checked out Alice and everything's fine."

"When do you think the calf will be born?" asked Penny.

"I can't tell, Pen. The doc said in about a week."

"I hope it doesn't happen when we're at school."

"Gosh, me too."

Penny chattered about the pageant and the kids who were acting in the play that would be presented to the student body on Friday afternoon. "That's just in five days!"

"I know," said Annette, "and then we'll be off for a whole two weeks … I can't wait."

The bus was on time this morning. As they climbed on, Pete grinned and waved to them from the back of the bus, where he sat alone. Annette and Penny swung into the seat across from him.

Pete didn't talk much. He usually just sat there, watching the girls and smiling back when Annette smiled at him. *Why is he always so shy?* Annette thought to herself. *Oh well …* She was just happy to be sitting near him.

It was a long day at school. Mondays were always boring. Penny had to stay after for practice, so Annette rode the school bus home and this time Pete sat beside her in the seat.

They talked about their Geometry assignment, and then Pete asked Annette again about her cow.

"Oh, she's doing fine," said Annette. "Do you wanna come over and have a look?"

Blushing, Pete smiled and stared into his lap. "Aw, that's

okay. I can't stop by today anyway. We have so much work to do. I wish my dad would hire some help, but he really can't afford to pay anyone."

Annette felt sorry for him. She knew the situation at the Randt farm was grim. They were a family struggling to survive. At least Mr. Randt had not caved in to Earl Warner's offer to buy him out and turn the old Anderson place—which was what their farm was called before the Randts moved there—into a development for recreational homes.

The bus stopped to let the Bronson sisters off at the corner of Tower Drive. Pete was looking out the window and he suddenly grabbed Annette's arm. "Hey, look."

Annette turned her attention out the window. "What?"

Pete pointed through the woods. On a far hill, off Tower Drive, stood the old abandoned water tower, now rusty and decrepit. The tower had been a relic from a century ago and had given the road its name. Annette strained to see what Pete was showing her.

"There," he said. "See that wisp of smoke?"

Annette had to look really hard, but then she saw a small curl of gray smoke over the tree line, next to the old tower. "Well, it sure looks like smoke, doesn't it?"

"Yeah. I wonder who's there."

"Maybe somebody's camping," said Annette.

"I don't know who'd be camping out in this cold weather," said Pete.

"Hunters? Maybe poachers." Annette's blue eyes lit up.

Pete laughed. "I doubt it. You and Penny cleaned all the poachers out of Jackson County last month."

"Maybe it's just somebody burning trash." Annette shrugged as the doors squealed shut and the school bus rolled on ahead.

When they came to the Randt farm on Gaston Road, Pete got off the bus. Annette waved goodbye to him, then sat back in the seat to think as the bus driver circled back up Tower Drive toward Ogden Road, where she lived.

It did seem strange to her to see that wisp of smoke coming from the vicinity of the old tower. She and Penny had talked about exploring the tower on more than one occasion. She had always been intrigued by it, for some reason. It was on state land, but they had to cross private property to get to it, and they had never had the nerve to walk over there.

"Some day," Annette said to herself as she gathered together her things before the bus stopped at the corner of Ogden Road.

Ruby Foley was not going to have a merry Christmas this year. She was devastated by the situation around her. How could her life have turned upside down so suddenly? A month ago, she had been carefree, a 13-year-old eighth grader, surrounded by her friends, admired by her teachers, and protected by an older brother.

"But now look at me," she pouted as she opened a can of tuna fish with one of those C-ration gadgets that wasn't much bigger than a razor blade.

It was growing dark in the musty little trailer that belonged to Uncle Will. She stood at the small discolored sink that was cluttered with dirty cups, plates and flatware.

The man who was her mother's brother was clean enough and not grubby like most, but he had a few things to learn about keeping house. He hung his clothes in heaps over all the chairs. They took up room on the sofa and the little dinette table that left hardly any passing space in the miniature kitchen.

He never made his bed either. Dad had always impressed on them to make their beds up first thing in the morning. But as much as she resented having to stay here, she shuddered when she started thinking about the alternative. The memory of what had happened last week was too horrible to think about. She wouldn't let herself dwell on it.

She reached up and opened one of the metal cupboards and pulled out a small white bowl that had a crack in the bottom. A spoon in the bottom of the sink wasn't too dirty, so she used it to scrape the tuna out into the bowl, then went to the little icebox that Uncle Will used to keep his milk cold — and other things. He had a tiny jar of Hellmann's that she used with the tuna. She couldn't find any pickles. That just added to her misery.

It was five o'clock. She knew that her uncle would be coming home from work soon. She found the loaf of Wonder bread on the counter top and removed a white slice, then smeared a layer of the tuna concoction onto it.

Uncle Will had some apple cider in the icebox. After she poured herself some into one of his chipped coffee mugs, she sat down at the tiny table, which rattled because it wasn't sturdy, and ate her supper.

She had been here now for five days. Where was Terry? He hadn't returned. He'd said he would, but he hadn't said *when*. Ruby recalled the day — last Thursday — when Uncle Will had met them at the bus depot and brought them to his trailer park. She was still pretty much traumatized. She knew that Uncle Will knew the story of what had happened because Terry would have explained it to him. But she didn't like the fact that her brother had *left* her here.

Uncle Will had been nice enough, though. He was what Terry called "eccentric." When she asked her brother what that word meant, he'd said, "Different ... but in a *good* way."

"Why can't I go with you?" Ruby had whined when Terry explained to her what he had to do.

"You'll be safe here," he promised her. Then, when she started blubbering because of the bad memories that were still fresh, he had hugged her to him and comforted her. "Ruby, don't worry. Uncle Will isn't going to tell anyone. You need to stay inside the trailer, though. You can't go anywhere. Do you understand? Tell me you will obey the rules."

Now he was sounding like Dad with his *rules*. She nodded through her tears. "Just tell me where you're going," she begged.

He shook his head. "Probably on a wild goose chase," he said. "But I'll be back. I promise."

"When?"

"In a week or two."

"But ... what about Christmas?"

Terry had frowned. "I'm sorry, Ruby. I know what Christmas means to you. This year is going to be a bit different. But next year ... if things work out the way I hope they do, next year's Christmas could be better than all the Christmases we've ever had."

"You *are* coming back?" Ruby trembled.

"I'll be back. I promise."

Remembering his words before he went out the door, Ruby recalled that Dad had said that as well. He had promised to come back, but he hadn't.

In July, her mother had gotten the letter from the War Department, telling them that Major Bob Foley's plane had gone down in the jungles near Hanoi and he was considered "Missing in Action."

At first, they had believed there was hope, and that he would be found. They needed to believe that he was alive. But as the weeks passed into months, without any confirmation, it began to look hopeless.

By Thanksgiving, Mom was so filled with grief and anguish that she felt certain he was dead and not in some P.O.W. camp. Then Mom had started drinking again—something she had overcome earlier in her life—and then, just a couple of weeks ago, she took all those sleeping pills.

And now Mom was dead.

The Social Services people had come and taken Ruby and her brother to foster homes. Since they had no close relatives, they had no choice. Grandma Foley had passed away last spring. Ruby had no cousins — no one, just her brother Terry, the *best brother in the world*. Yet the social workers from the State had found it to be in everyone's best interest to separate the two of them.

Against major protests, Ruby had gone to live with Betty and Colonel Ralph Somers, who took in foster kids now and then. Ralph had been in the Air Force and Betty was a quiet, thin, rather timid woman who didn't interact with Ruby much.

Terry had been placed in a home with one of his teachers in high school, who had offered to help them out. They couldn't take Ruby, unfortunately. The wife worked outside the home and Social Services didn't like kids being by themselves, especially after traumatic events.

Footsteps startled Ruby from her thoughts. Chewing her sandwich, she turned around in her seat as Uncle Will came through the door to the trailer. He was a short but solid man with blondish hair, thick white eyebrows, a white mustache and a round nose. He resembled Ruby's and Terry's mom quite a bit. They had the same coloring, and Mom had been round-shaped and not very tall. Her blondish hair had turned white a couple of years ago and her face had been drawn and wrinkled from worry. Uncle Will's hair was thin and he combed it forward to try and hide his receding hairline.

He set a paper bag with some groceries down on the counter next to the sink. "Bought some cereal," he said as he removed his coat and threw it onto the sofa, on top of some other clothes. "I hope you like Post Toasties."

Ruby couldn't answer with her mouth full.

Uncle Will started taking things out of the bag. "Myself, I prefer Trix. But ... Trix are for kids." He handed her a bag of

Red Dot potato chips. "Here ... to go with your supper."

Ruby took the bag. "Thank you," she said.

"Heard from your brother today?" asked her uncle. He ran the faucet to wash his hands.

"No, sir."

"I'm no *sir*," Uncle Will said in a low voice. "Where did you get all this 'sir' business, anyway?"

"My dad." Ruby wiped her mouth with the back of her hand.

"Of course ... the United States Marine."

"No, he was an Air Force major." Suddenly, the mention of her missing father triggered a blast of ugly, recent memories. Terry had warned her not to go there.

"Oh, that's right." Uncle Will cleared his throat and wiped his hands with a dirty towel. He never got too excited about anything, she noticed. He seemed to lack emotions, which Ruby found unusual, since her dad had been so disciplined and high strung, and her mother had been what her grandmother had called a "drama queen." Grandma had always warned Ruby that she would turn into a "drama queen" like her mother. "*Settle down, girl. You're gonna be a drama queen like your mama. Hush now and be a little lady.*"

There were long silences between Ruby and Uncle Will. He didn't seem too bothered by the fact that she didn't ask for anything or talk to him much. She just thought he was kind of strange, going about his life in this small trailer as if she had always been there, like a fixture or a piece of furniture that he maneuvered around while going about his routine.

She never saw him laugh, or get mad or get upset. He liked to sit and watch his small black-and-white TV set, or sit in the easy chair, still heaped with his clothes, and sometimes he read his books about a man named John Muir, who had something to do with the national parks.

There were lots of picture books around that Ruby

thumbed through, most of which were about places such as Canyonlands in Utah, Yellowstone National Park and Yosemite in California. She especially liked looking at the Redwoods.

She knew that Uncle Will worked for the Wisconsin Department of Natural Resources. In the wintertime he did some kind of office work. In summer he was a park ranger. She didn't know which parks, though. He didn't talk about himself at all. He was simply a quiet man who liked staying in this small trailer, living a very boring life.

"Tomorrow I get a day off," said Uncle Will, eating the rest of the tuna concoction right out of the bowl with a spoon.

Ruby looked over at him with interest.

"I thought you might like to get out of the house. I could take you to the roller skating rink."

Ruby sighed. "I don't know, Uncle Will. Terry said it was important for me to stay right here."

He didn't look at her. "You're bored stiff here, Ruby. I don't want you going crazy on me."

Ruby felt a tear forming in her eye. She was afraid to speak. She did feel terribly confined, but more than that, she was afraid. Terry had made it clear that she wasn't to go out in public and be seen. Someone might recognize her.

Even though Madison, Wisconsin was well over a thousand miles from her home in Colorado Springs, she knew the police had been informed and posters with her picture on it might turn up in a place as big as Madison. She didn't want to see her brother go to jail.

6

A Promotion

Pete was absent from school the next day. He wasn't on the school bus. As the driver made the turn off Tower Drive, Annette remembered the smoke Pete had seen near the old water tower. She told Penny about it.

"Ooh, sounds like another mystery brewing." Penny grinned.

Annette frowned. "Come on, Pen. It's no mystery. Someone was either camping out in the woods or burning trash or something."

Penny looked out the window. All they could see were the woods with their snow-covered limbs. The top of the old tower poked through about a quarter mile away from the road. "But who would be out there at this time of year? Maybe we should go check it out, Annette."

"You're nuts," said Annette, but she didn't reveal to her friend that she had already thought of that. She had been trying to figure out how they could get through those woods and hike through the snow to get to the water tower.

She had always figured they would explore it in the summer. They would have gotten around to it last summer, but hadn't had time. They had been too busy with 4H and trying to earn money so they could a buy a horse. Then the trip to Colorado had happened in August, right before school started.

Annette fell into a reverie of the wonderful vacation to the Cochetopa Hills near Gunnison, where she and Penny had stayed at the Mitchell ranch and gone horse-back riding with Mandy Mitchell, an adventurous 16-year-old blonde who was used to getting her way. Mandy had led them into the forbidden hills, where they had gotten into trouble numerous times. Mandy had been determined to uncover a mystery that involved an old mountain man named Jebb Hickory.

"When do you wanna go?" Annette asked.

Penny stared at her. "What are you talking about?"

"The old tower. When do you want to go explore it?"

Penny smoothed her long dark hair and laughed. "Oh Annette, are you serious?"

"Well, you're the one who brought it up. Do you have to go to practice again tonight?"

Penny nodded. "Yup. All week, I'm afraid."

"Darn." Annette looked out the window. The bus had reached the highway and was heading into town. "It looks like we'll have to wait until the weekend."

"So you want to do it?" asked Penny.

"Maybe."

"But you said yourself that the smoke Pete saw was probably nothing."

Annette sighed. "You're right, Pen. It's just that ... I have a feeling. I need to go and find out."

"Well, okay, let's do it Saturday," said Penny.

"Then it's settled," said Annette. Suddenly, she wasn't so depressed about Pete not being on the bus. She had a goal now ... a *purpose* ... to find out what was going on at the old abandoned tower.

On Wednesday afternoon, when she got home from school, Annette called Pete's house to find out why he had been absent again. He had missed two days.

"Hi, Annette," said a groggy-sounding Pete when he picked up the telephone.

"Pete, are you sick?" she asked.

He coughed, then said, "Kind of."

"What do you have?"

"Just a cold," said Pete. "It's nothing, really. Mom made us stay home yesterday and today. But I think I'll be in school tomorrow."

Annette heard Pete's mother in the background, yelling something.

Pete muffled his voice and said, "Of course it depends on how I am."

"Oh Pete, I'm sorry you don't feel well," said Annette. "Is Mark sick too?"

"Yeah, about five of us stayed home from school. Addie's got it, and so do Linda and Jeff."

"Gee, that's too bad."

"How's Alice?" asked Pete. He sniffed.

"Oh, the same," said Annette. "I think the calf will be coming any day now."

After a short pause, Pete said, "Annette, if I don't go to school tomorrow, could you bring some of my homework to me?"

Annette brightened. "Of course, Pete. I'd be happy to."

"Aw, thanks. I don't wanna get behind, especially in Geometry."

"I know what you mean."

They talked a short while longer, and then Annette had to go milk Elizabeth before it got too dark. "I hope you'll be in school by Friday, at least, because Penny's playing the piano in that Christmas pageant in front of the whole school."

Pete perked up. "I wouldn't miss it." She could tell he was smiling.

When they hung up, Annette felt it had cheered Pete up for her to call him. Well, it was a start anyway, and if he wasn't in school tomorrow, she'd get to bring his homework to him. She wanted to visit the Randts again and perhaps see baby Laura and all those darling Randt children.

She sighed as she went out to the barn to do the milking. How lucky Pete was to have a big family. With all those brothers and sisters, she could only imagine how magical it must be on Christmas morning. A few times she had spent Christmas with the Duncans, while her mother had to work at the hospital, and having family made the holidays much more special.

"Oh, if only ..." Annette moaned.

The bell on the door of Mr. Brown's store tinkled as Terry entered on Thursday morning. No one was in the store except its owner, who looked up from behind the counter and smiled in recognition. "Well, young man ... are you going to take me up on my offer?"

Terry walked in and removed his stocking cap. He didn't have the pack on his back this time. He smiled. "There's a half a cord cut and split. All I need now is a way to get it to you, Mr. Brown."

"Half a cord, eh? That's pretty quick work, I'd say."

"I could get you a lot more, if I had the use of a chainsaw."

"Tell ya what," said Mr. Brown. "You've earned my trust. I'll let you take my McCullough. It's greased up and ready to use. Why don't you take my pick-up and haul the wood back here? Soon as it's unloaded in the wood shed, I'll pay ya."

Terry looked at Mr. Brown in astonishment.

"What's the matter?" asked Mr. Brown. "You're old

enough to drive, aren't ya?"

"Well, yeah… I'll turn 17 in March."

"And you've used a chainsaw before?"

Terry nodded.

"Driver's license?" asked Mr. Brown.

Terry frowned, then reached into one coat pocket and then the other. He looked over at the storekeeper. "I seem to have … I must have left my driver's license in my backpack."

Mr. Brown wasn't paying any attention. He got a set of keys out from under the counter near the cash register, then handed them to Terry. "Here. Take the truck. It's got half a tank of gas in it. Should get you there and back."

"Thanks, Mr. Brown." Terry took the keys and looked around at the shelves in the store.

"Are you hungry?" asked Mr. Brown. When Terry didn't answer right away, the storekeeper lifted the cover on a tray of freshly baked doughnuts. "Here, help yourself, boy. You look like you could use a cup of coffee, too."

"If you've got some, that would be great," said Terry.

"You didn't tell me if you found a place to stay," said Mr. Brown, handing him a large chocolate frosted doughnut on a napkin. He went over to his coffee pot, plugged into the wall behind the counter, and filled a mug with the hot black drink.

"Oh, I did," said Terry. He took a bite of the doughnut. "Thanks a lot, Mr. Brown." He chewed, then swallowed. "This is really good."

"Mrs. Brown made them early this morning." He brought the hot cup of coffee over to Terry, who took a seat next to the door. "In fact, it was Mrs. Brown who came up with the idea of giving you the job of cutting some firewood for us." Mr. Brown was obviously in the mood for conversation this morning. He glanced out the window. "I think we're in for a bad winter this year. It's been so busy in this store, I just didn't have a lot of time to cut wood this fall."

A blue Jeep pulled up in front of the store and two people got out—a thin, long-haired man and a heavyset woman.

"Oh, here come those darn hippies again," grumbled Mr. Brown.

Terry's eyebrows shot up as he watched the tall guy with greasy black hair and a scraggly beard walk into the store wearing very tight blue jeans and a denim jacket. The woman had frizzy red hair and wore a floor-length skirt underneath her heavy winter coat. He realized he had seen that woman before. Where? Then he remembered ... at the post office in town last week.

Mr. Brown didn't speak to the couple. Instead, he went behind the counter and pretended to be busy. Terry sat and ate his doughnut and sipped at the coffee, but kept his eyes on the two people. They stayed close to one another as they roamed the aisles, whispering to themselves.

The girl noticed him, but she didn't seem to remember that he had been in line at the post office when she had gone off about the war in Vietnam. The two of them picked out a few items and brought them to the front, and then the man went back to get something else. The woman looked around, then disappeared into the store's restroom.

An old brown pickup truck pulled up in front of the store next. A farmer in overalls and a tattered coat got out and came inside the store. "Mornin', Fred," the farmer greeted Mr. Brown.

"Mr. Randt, good morning. How's the wife and that new baby girl?"

"Oh, they're gettin' along just fine, thanks. But we need some cough syrup and some Vicks. Got a half dozen sick kids missin' school this week."

"Oh, that's too bad, Mr. Randt. I'm sorry to hear that." Mr. Brown stepped out from behind the counter to lead his customer over to the shelf where he kept some medicines.

The hippie man had grabbed a magazine at the counter and was paging through it, waiting for his partner. Terry finished eating the doughnut and used the napkin to wipe his lip, then downed the rest of the coffee. He thought he'd better get started to bring the load of wood back to Mr. Brown's Store.

Suddenly, the red-haired, heavyset woman came out of the restroom and smiled at her partner reading the magazine. They nodded at each other, and then they dropped a couple dollar bills on the counter and left the store, not bothering to wait for any change.

Mr. Randt, the farmer, followed the storekeeper over to the cash register. His eyes swept toward Terry and he nodded in greeting.

"Oh, say ... Mr. Randt, I want you to meet this young man. Terry's his name. He's helping the wife and me out by cutting a load of wood for us."

Terry stood and faced Mr. Randt, then extended his right hand. Mr. Randt shook it. "Glad to know ya, Terry."

"This here's Mr. Randt. He's got a dairy farm." Mr. Brown then quickly added, "Terry's needing a job. I don't suppose you'd need any help now, would ya?"

Mr. Randt stroked his whiskery chin and looked Terry over from head to toe. "Well, now ... that's a thought, actually." He stepped back as if to consider the idea. "What's your name, young man?"

"Terry Knutson."

"Where you from?"

Terry swallowed, but remained composed. "Oh, here and there. I spent some time out West."

"Is that right?" The farmer kept studying the boy.

Mr. Brown grabbed up the dollar bills lying on the counter to stick in his cash box.

"You're a drifter? What brings you to this part of the

state?" asked Mr. Randt.

Terry winced. "I'm doing a little family research," he revealed. "You know, visiting cemeteries." He then had a thought. "I'm working on a research paper ... for school."

"College boy?" Mr. Randt's eyebrows shot up. "You look kinda young for that."

Mr. Brown interjected. "Terry's a hard worker, Mr. Randt. Maybe you could use him on your farm for a few days."

Mr. Randt sighed. "I know we could," he said. "It's just ... I can't pay much."

"He'll do anything," said Mr. Brown.

"Room and board? Plus ten dollars a week?" proposed Mr. Randt.

Terry brightened at the idea of having a warm place to stay and meals, even if it was only for a week or so. It would give him a base and he could spend his free time doing his research. He regretted that he'd had to fib a little. But his alibi was not entirely false. He was looking for a relative, after all. And so he agreed. Mr. Randt paid for his supplies, then told Mr. Brown to bring the young man to his farm later that day, after the wood had been delivered.

Mr. Brown stood beside Terry as they watched the farmer get into his brown pickup and leave. "I guess you'd better get that wood, young man. You've just been promoted."

7

Pete's Homework

"You want false eyelashes for Christmas?" Penny guffawed as they stood at their locker after lunch, before the bell rang for fifth hour. She had Annette's Christmas Wish List in her hand.

"I don't know why I wrote that down." Annette felt a crimson wave on her cheeks.

Nancy Marshall and Debbie Kelton—both sophomores—were standing next to them, discussing the boys they currently liked. Debbie had caught what Penny said and poked Annette in fun. "I have a pair of false eyelashes at home. They're not anything great, believe me."

"You don't need them," said Nancy. "Not with your beautiful eyes, Annette."

"Hey, I think Tim has Tommy James and The Shondelles," said Penny. "But it would be groovy if your mom got you The Cream."

"Oh, I *love* The Cream," squealed Debbie.

Penny shrieked when she came to the last item on Annette's list. "A *boy!*" She waved the paper in front of their friends. "Annette actually wants a *boy* for Christmas."

"Well, who doesn't?" Nancy stood with a hand on her hip.

Penny read it out loud: "A Boy — 16 or older, and taller, with a nice *crop of hair!*" She laughed and the others joined in. Annette had no choice but to laugh too. She was embarrassed as could be, but at least no one who mattered could hear. Pete was home again, sick. She looked forward to getting his assignments from all his teachers. She had already asked Tim to give her a ride home from school, and he had agreed to take her over to the Randts' farm.

Just then, Lisa Kowalski from FFA passed by and stopped when she saw Annette and Penny.

"Scott said your piano playing is amazing," Lisa told Penny. "I'm looking forward to the Christmas pageant tomorrow."

"Oh ... well, thanks, Lisa." Penny suddenly blushed, now that all the attention was directed at her.

"I think he's got a crush on you," Lisa whispered, then smiled and walked on down the hall.

Everyone had heard. Nancy, Debbie and Annette all stared at Penny with their mouths open, then burst out laughing. "Scott Kowalski has a crush on Penny Duncan!" Nancy shouted.

"Shhh... *shhhh*... you *guys!*" Penny cowered inside her locker as some senior boys passed by. Other kids looked in their direction. Just then, the bell rang and Nancy and Debbie hurried away.

Annette giggled. "Saved by the bell." She took the Wish List from Penny, then reached for the books she needed for her afternoon classes. "Don't worry, Pen. Your secret is safe with me."

"He's a nerd," said Penny. "Oh my gosh, what if this gets around? What will Steve Newton think?"

Annette went to the gymnasium. She had Phy. Ed. fifth period and they were playing girls' basketball. Basketball was not her favorite sport, but she enjoyed the exercise, which perked her up for History class and then the dreaded Geometry. After class, she got Pete's assignment from Mr. Raymond, and then went to all of Pete's other teachers to collect homework for him.

Tim met Annette in the senior hall after most the students had cleared out of the building. Penny was at pageant practice, and they could hear the music coming from the auditorium. Tim was just saying goodbye to a cute junior girl — one of Tim's many admirers.

He smiled broadly when Annette approached. "Hi, Annette."

"Oh, Tim, thanks for giving me a ride over to Pete's."

"Hey, I'm happy to do it." He grabbed the heavy load of books from her arms. "Here, let me."

She fastened her coat and then followed Penny's dark-haired brother down the hall and out the doors. They walked carefully through the icy parking lot, where Tim's blue Chevelle was waiting. Annette almost slipped a couple of times. She climbed into the passenger seat while Tim dumped all of the books and papers behind the driver's seat. Then he got in and started the engine.

"Is Alice showing any signs of giving birth yet?" Tim asked as they left the town of Ravensville and headed for the highway.

"I don't think so," said Annette. "What should I be looking for?"

"Well, she'll probably freshen. That'll be the first sign," said Tim.

"You mean, she'll start giving milk again?" asked Annette.

"Right. Before cows give birth, they start lactating ... usually twenty-four hours before, but sometimes their udders start filling with milk two or three weeks ahead."

"Will she lay down?"

"Not necessarily," said Tim. "Most cows give birth standing up."

"Gee, you know so much about it."

Tim caught her look of wonder and smiled. "We have a lot of calves at our farm, you know."

Annette knew that was true. "How will I know it's Alice's time?"

Tim smiled. "You'll know. She might start fidgeting and straining a little. You might see her sides sink in. Her water bag might hang down. It usually appears first ... before the calf is born."

"Well, I'm looking forward to this," said Annette. "When Elizabeth and Alice had their first calves over a year ago, your dad still had them, remember?"

"Yeah, I remember," said Tim. "You and Penny were still teeny boppers then." He grinned.

Annette blushed, not knowing how to respond to his teasing.

"I'd like it if you'd give me a call at the first sign," said Tim. He looked at her in such a special way that Annette felt goose bumps erupting on her neck and arms. She remembered that Pete, too, wanted to help her with the calving. But Tim lived closer and had a lot more experience. "I will," she told him.

They turned off the highway where Browns' Store was the first building, then went down Ogden Road and passed the Duncan farm on the left, then Annette's house a short ways farther, on the right. The Vetter car was gone, which meant that Annette's mother had gone to work. Tim drove on down to the junction at Tower Drive, where there was a stop sign, and which was also the girls' bus stop.

"Hey, Tim, just a minute," said Annette when he stopped to wait for a car to pass. "Before you take me to Pete's house, can we go down that way?" She pointed off to the left. "I want to see something."

Tim glanced at her with a puzzled look, but shrugged. "Okay." He signaled for the turn. "What is it you wanna see?"

"I want to drive past the old tower," she said.

"Oh? Okay." Tim turned the wheel and started slowly down Tower Drive.

Annette knew he was waiting for an explanation. "On Monday, when we were riding home from school, Pete saw some smoke coming out of the woods by the old tower."

"Really?" Tim did not seem impressed with the news. "Probably a camper."

"Probably," agreed Annette. "I just wanted to see if it's still there."

"The smoke?"

"Well, yeah ... and maybe if there's any tracks. Like if a car parked along the woods ... we'd see some tracks."

They rode a ways until the high part of the tower came into view over the tree line. Tim stopped the car and they cruised slowly along the shoulder of the county road.

"I don't see any smoke today," said Annette.

"There's been some activity here, though," said Tim. "Look." He pointed out Annette's window and she saw where the snow had been disturbed alongside the road. A vehicle had been there several times, it looked like, and they could see some footprints and some scattered limbs off pine trees.

Annette studied the area closely. It looked like there was a path of footprints that led into the woods. She and Penny could follow that path when they came to explore on Saturday. The snow wasn't that deep that they couldn't penetrate those woods on foot. She needed to know what was at the old tower and find out if anyone had been camping there ... or possibly poaching.

Tim turned around and drove in the other direction, toward Gaston Road, where the Randt farm was. They arrived ten minutes later, and Tim decided to wait in the car with the engine running while Annette gathered up Pete's homework and made her way to the front porch of the old yellow farmhouse.

She could hear kids hollering inside and a television blaring. When she knocked on the door, Kay Randt, Pete's oldest sister, answered and smiled broadly. Kay, who was 12, was blonde with a ponytail and brown eyes. "Annette!" she cried with delight. "Hey, everyone ... Annette is here."

Embarrassed, Annette stepped into the warm dining room. Young Billy Randt, a blond-haired, boisterous 6-year-old, barged in from the adjoining room, where some of the kids had been watching afternoon cartoons. Addie, who was 8, brought the youngest boy, Eddie, who was only 2. They all laughed and cheered at the sight of her.

"Ma! Annette's here!"

Annette looked around, expecting Pete to appear, but instead Mrs. Randt stepped out of the kitchen door, dressed in an apron and wearing a scarf over her dark hair. Her green eyes seemed to twinkle and she smiled broadly. "Hello, Annette. So nice you could come. Don't get too close to the children now. Addie, we don't want to give Annette your cold."

Coughing sounds came from the other room. Annette could see Linda's head peering up at her from the sofa in the family room. Little Jeff was fussing and running around, wreaking havoc.

"Pete's just coming in now," said Mrs. Randt with a glance out the window. "He's sick still, but he had to help out in the barn."

"Is the baby sleeping?" asked Annette. She had hoped she'd get to see the new infant.

"Laura's upstairs in her crib," explained Kay. "Want me to get her?"

"Oh, don't disturb her," said Annette. "I just wanted to bring Pete his homework."

"That was so very thoughtful," said Mrs. Randt.

Annette glanced out the window. Although it was just starting to get darker, she could see Pete, dressed in a heavy coat, ear muffs and baggy jeans, headed for the house. Behind him was another fellow, a taller, more slender young man dressed in a bulky coat and wearing thick gloves. He wore a stocking cap and had medium-length blond hair and whiskers.

Waving to Tim in the car, Pete climbed the porch steps and stamped his boots before entering the house. His companion was right behind him. Pete grinned when he caught sight of Annette. "Hi!"

"Pete, are you sure you should be out in that cold?" Annette chided him.

In response, Pete let out a loud, raspy cough, but covered his mouth. "It's okay. I'm fine. I just had to help out a little. My dad wanted me to show Terry what to do."

The young blond man who had come in after Pete stood there, studying Annette. She gasped when she met his eyes. "I know you," said Annette.

"You do?" Pete looked baffled and turned to their hired help.

Terry smiled. "We met at the post office," he explained in a calm voice. Then he cocked his head. "Is that right?" He looked at Annette. "At least I *think* that's where I saw you ... in line that day ... with all those packages."

"Yes." Annette laughed. She turned to Pete. "Lisa Kowalski and I had to mail all those care packages out that the Future Farmers club got ready."

"Oh ... okay." Pete wore a worried look on his face, but immediately wiped it away with a smile. "Well, this is Terry Knutson, our new farm hand."

"At least for a while." Terry removed his dirty, oversized

gloves, and reached out to shake Annette's hand. She shifted the books so she could shake his hand, which felt warm and strong.

"Good to meet you, Terry."

"Annette, you can put those books down on the table," directed Mrs. Randt.

From upstairs they heard a baby crying. Addie set Eddie down on the floor and marched toward the stairway in the hall. "Laura's awake! I'll go get her."

"I'll help you," said Kay.

Mrs. Randt put her hands on her hips. "Change her before you bring her down, please, Addie."

"We will, Mom."

Annette remembered how caring the Randt girls were toward their younger brothers and sisters. Addie, who was a little more emotional than her other sisters, seemed to be following in her sister Linda's footsteps as far as being "the little mother" to the babies in the family.

"Can you stay awhile? I'll put on some hot chocolate," offered Mrs. Randt.

"No, Tim's waiting for me out in the car," said Annette. "He has to get home to do the milking."

"Tell him to come in," begged Mrs. Randt.

"Tim is your ... *brother?*" asked Terry.

"Oh no, he's a neighbor," explained Annette with a smile.

"Tim Duncan," explained Pete. "You'll like him. He's cool."

"And you are also Pete's ... *neighbor?*" asked Terry.

"You could say that," said Pete with a chuckle.

"Pete and Cousin Luke took Annette to the Homecoming dance," blurted out Linda, who was 9 and had suddenly emerged from the television room, wrapped in a blanket. She blotted the end of her nose with a tissue.

Annette blushed. She didn't know what to say about that

remark. "I live down on Ogden Road, across from the Duncan farm," she explained.

"Oh yeah, Ogden Road. That's where Mr. Brown's store is."

"And the Vetters live about a mile and a half from there," said Pete.

"Terry, why don't you wash up in the bathroom?" Mrs. Randt nodded toward the stairway. "You could use a hot shower before we sit down to supper, and I fixed up your room in the basement. It's not much, but it stays fairly warm down there, next to the boiler room."

Terry didn't speak right away. A startled look had appeared on his face and he continued to stare at Annette. She looked at him curiously, wondering why he was suddenly so flabbergasted.

Then, with a slight shake of his head, he recovered and murmured a thank you, then excused himself and slipped off toward the bathroom to clean up.

Pete noticed Annette's puzzled look. "It's okay. He's harmless." Pete explained how Mr. Brown had referred Terry to them as a hired hand. "Apparently he did some odd jobs for Mr. Brown, who says he's down on his luck. Dad says he seems trustworthy and I think he's really a good guy."

"Well, I certainly hope so," agreed Annette. She remembered how shabby Reid Anderson, their last hired help, had looked when she had met him at Thanksgiving. No one would have suspected Reid of being an accomplice to Earl Warner's shenanigans, or even friendly with the poachers who had used the Randts' land and other's property to illegally take game. They had even poached on the Vetters' forty acres.

She also remembered how the boy, Terry, had confronted that hippie woman in the post office almost a week ago. She wondered what his story was … where he came from.

She didn't get a chance to find out, because after she

explained to Pete about his assignments, and the other kids were getting back to their fun, Addie brought the new baby downstairs. Mrs. Randt came out of the kitchen and took baby Laura in her arms, then came over to show Annette.

"Here she is," said Mrs. Randt, pulling the receiving blanket away from the baby's face. The infant had a few dark curls and deep blue eyes. A few tiny bubbles formed on the corner of her cherub pink mouth and she fussed a little, obviously growing hungry.

"Oh, she's lovely," breathed Annette. "She's grown a lot since I last saw her. Hi, little Laura ..."

The Randt girls fussed over their new baby sister. After another minute, Annette remembered that Tim was waiting for her out in the car. She was sure he needed to get home, and she had chores of her own to do before it got any darker. She hastily told everyone goodbye and then ran out to the car.

"I'm sorry, Tim," said Annette as she climbed in and slammed the door shut. "I didn't mean to be in there so long."

"It's okay, Annette." Tim had been fiddling with his car radio and The Cream was playing *The Sunshine of Your Love*.

"Oh, I just love that song," she crooned as they backed down the snowy driveway.

Tim grinned at her, then drove back toward their road. As the music played, Tim turned up the volume. Annette soon got lost in the song. But she kept seeing the attractive face of the boy, Terry, in her mind, and suddenly she had so many questions about him that she could hardly think about anything else.

Who *was* Terry Knutson? What was he doing in Ravensville, and how had he managed to go to work for the Randts? She couldn't wait to tell Penny.

8

The Christmas Pageant

The next morning was Friday. Annette was up at her usual early hour, excited because this was going to be the last day of school in 1968. Christmas vacation would start after classes got out that afternoon. She looked forward to no homework for two whole weeks, and possibly getting to go back to bed and sleep another hour after the milking and other chores were done.

The phone rang when she came back into the house. Her mother was still in bed, so Annette picked it up quickly, so it would not disturb Mrs. Vetter. "Hello?"

"Annette!" It was Penny.

"Oh, hi, Pen."

"Tim's gonna drive us to school this morning."

"Great!" Then she added, "How come?"

"Well, I've got stuff I need to take for the pageant this afternoon. Plus he said he wanted to check on Alice. How's she doing, anyway?"

"Nothing's changed," said Annette. "But, yeah ... that would be great if he had a look at her."

"We'll be over at seven-thirty," said Penny.

After she hung up the phone, Annette got Ginger's kibble

out of the lower cupboard, filled his dish and gave him some fresh water in his bowl. The collie gently licked the back of her hand before he bent over his food and quietly began to consume it. "Such a good boy you are," Annette crooned. The long, thick, red tail swished back and forth a couple of times in response.

Next, she put some water in the coffee pot, then measured some already ground beans into the basket and plugged the percolator in. She knew her mother would appreciate having fresh coffee waiting for her once she got up.

Annette sighed, opening the refrigerator door to get out a couple of fresh eggs. Her mother was still kind of depressed. The house seemed empty lately, even when they both were home. Mrs. Vetter used to like to chat all the time. Lately, she'd been too quiet. Even her knitting had been neglected. She slept longer too, which worried Annette considerably.

Tim's Chevelle pulled into the Vetters' driveway promptly at seven-thirty. Annette was dressed for school, in a red, long-sleeved sweater over a white cotton turtleneck. She had found an emerald green skirt in her closet and decided her choice had been appropriate for the anticipation of Christmas. She pulled on her coat and grabbed her purse and homework bag. Ginger wanted to come out, to see who had arrived outside the house, but she made him stay inside.

"Mom will be up real soon, Ginger. Stay!"

Both Tim and Penny climbed out of the car, which they left running in the cold weather.

"Let's have a look at Alice," said Tim with a grin.

Penny had white pantyhose on and a white skirt and shoes beneath her tan winter coat. She followed them on the snow-packed path to the barn.

Both Elizabeth and Alice were standing in their stalls, chewing their cuds. Tim went over to examine the pregnant cow, and Annette told Penny about her visit to the Randts'.

"I wonder if Pete'll be in school today," said Penny.

"He said he was still not feeling well, but *maybe*," Annette said hopefully. Then she added, "Did you know the Randts hired a guy to help out on the farm?"

"They did?" Penny's green eyes opened wide. "Who?"

"His name is Terry Knutson," said Annette. "But guess what? He was at the post office last week, on Friday afternoon. Remember when I helped Lisa take all those packages to mail to the soldiers in Vietnam?"

"Yes," said Penny. "So?" She looked puzzled.

"Well," said Annette, "do you remember me telling you that I had seen that hippie girl who was in Browns' Store last weekend? Remember her?"

"Oh yeah, the one that came out of the restroom."

"Terry was the boy in line at the post office who turned around and said something to her ... after that girl was so *mean*."

"Oh, yeah," said Penny. "Well, gosh ..."

Tim interrupted their conversation. "Hey, Alice is lactating."

"What?" Annette gasped. "She is?"

"It looks like her udders are filling up," said Tim. "I'd say she'll be going into labor real soon."

"Today?" Annette grew worried.

Tim shook his head. "Can't know for sure. But keep a close eye on her from now on."

"But, what if she goes into labor while I'm at school? And Mom's going to work this afternoon. No one will be here."

Penny shook her head. "She can't have the calf today ... not the day of the pageant!"

Tim grinned. "Most likely it won't be today." He led them back out to the car. "Come on ... we don't want to be late to school."

Penny chattered excitedly about the pageant and the play

while she and Annette sat in the back seat of the Chevelle. Tim drove up Ogden Road, then stopped at Browns' Store before pulling onto the highway.

"Why are we stopping here?" asked Penny.

"I'll just be a minute," said Tim.

"Won't we be late for school?" asked Annette.

"Nah, we still have plenty of time." Tim jumped out and left the car's engine running. He hurried inside the store and a minute later came back out with a small brown bag and some napkins.

"What did you get?" asked Penny.

Tim pulled a chocolate doughnut out of the bag. "I've been craving one of these all morning," he said. "It's one of Mrs. Brown's famous doughnuts." He took a big bite out of it.

"Hey! You pig!" blurted Penny. "That's not very nice ... eating in front of us!"

Tim turned around and made a face at his sister. Then he reached into the brown bag and pulled out another chocolate doughnut, which he handed to Annette. Then he took another big bite out of his.

"Ooh..." Annette accepted a napkin from Tim as her mouth began to water.

"That's not fair! Where's mine?" demanded Penny.

"Here, Pen, I'll share mine with you," said Annette.

Then Tim threw the bag at his sister, who caught it in mid-air. She looked inside and smirked, then pulled out her doughnut.

"Gee, thanks, Tim," said Annette. "These are awful good."

"I know," he said. "But be careful, please ... don't make a mess in my car."

"Too late!" squealed Penny as a hunk of chocolate fell to the floorboard.

Annette burst out laughing when she saw the look of

alarm on Tim's face. Then they quieted down and ate their doughnuts.

An old blue Jeep pulled in beside them, and they watched as a couple got out and walked into the store. Annette grabbed Penny's arm and tried to talk, but her mouth was full.

"What's wrong with *you*?" demanded Penny.

Finally, Annette wiped her mouth with the napkin. "That girl ... the one that just went into the store ..."

Penny craned her neck, but the two had already gone inside.

"It was that hippie chick," Annette explained. "This is the third time I've seen her this week."

Tim was listening as he finished his doughnut.

"They must live around here or something," remarked Penny.

After the girls were done with their doughnuts, Tim collected the trash and got out of the car to pitch it in the receptacle next to the store's entrance. As he was getting into the Chevelle again, the tall, thin man with scraggly, greasy dark hair and a beard came out and strutted to his car without looking at Tim.

Annette squinted her eyes. When Tim was behind the wheel again, they watched the fat girl come out, carrying a bag of potato chips and a six-pack of beer. "I'm sure I've seen that guy before," said Annette. "He looks really familiar."

Tim studied the couple in the Jeep beside them as it backed up, then spun around on the ice and shot away down Ogden Road. "Hmm," he said as he slowly pulled out of the parking lot. "I've seen him, too."

"Who is he?" asked Penny. She reached into her purse for her lipstick and a small compact mirror.

"I don't know his name," said Tim, "but I think I've seen him hanging around at the high school during noon hours and after classes."

Annette was interested. "He looks too old to be in high school."

"True," said Tim. "I've seen his Jeep parked in the school lot. Some of the loose kids know him. I've seen them hang out at his car, smoking and kidding around."

As they drove the rest of the way to school, Annette leaned forward and asked Tim, "Can you find out his name for me?"

"Why?" he asked.

"I've seen him before, I *know* I have," said Annette. Shivers went up her spine.

Penny's green eyes widened. "Do you suppose … Annette, are you thinking what *I'm* thinking?"

"What *are* you thinking?" Tim called out sarcastically.

"I don't know, Pen," Annette answered. "Something's not right with those two. I can feel it."

"Oooh, I was right," squealed Penny and clapped her hands. "Another mystery! We're gonna solve another mystery, aren't we, Annette?"

Reaching into her own purse, Annette found her tube of Palest Peach. "It's too early to tell," she said. "Hey, let me borrow your mirror a sec, Pen."

Tim glanced back at Annette and smiled, then winked at her. She smiled at him, then took the compact from her friend and drew some color back onto her lips.

The morning classes passed slowly for Annette. She wasn't surprised that Pete Randt hadn't come to school. She ate lunch in the cafeteria with her friends Debbie, Kathy and Nancy. Penny had gone to a final rehearsal during the noon hour. The pageant was being presented during seventh hour.

"Annette!" a male voice called from down the hallway.

Surprised, Annette looked up from where she had been digging through the bottom of her locker for her afternoon books and folders. There was Pete, dressed in a tan sweater, walking toward her, wearing a big grin on his face. "Hi, Pete!"

"I made it," he said. Immediately he turned aside and covered his mouth as he let out a cough.

"Are you sure you're feeling better?" She looked worried.

"So-so," he replied. "But I didn't want to miss the afternoon classes."

"The pageant is seventh hour," said Annette.

"I know. I didn't want to miss watching Penny play the piano." A big smile spread across his face.

"Well, I'm glad you're here," said Annette.

Pete coughed again, this time a longer, more congested expulsion. He looked at her sheepishly. "Sorry about that."

Annette let out a sigh. "Well, at least we get out of Geometry class."

"Good thing, too. I didn't catch up on my homework yet."

"It doesn't matter," said Annette. "Hey, how's that new guy working out? Terry ..."

Pete pulled out a large handkerchief from his pants pocket and blew his nose. "He's a good worker."

"What do you know about him?" asked Annette.

"Not too much," admitted Pete.

"But your dad hired him. You must know where he came from."

Pete turned and waved at one of the sophomore boys who was walking by and had greeted him. "Actually," he told Annette, "Terry's homeless."

"What!" Annette's blue eyes grew round. "You mean ... he doesn't have anywhere to stay?"

"He does now," said Pete.

"Oh, Pete, that's so sad. Where did he *used* to live?"

"He said he came from out West."

"Where? California?"

"I don't know, Annette. He doesn't seem to like to talk

about it. I know that. He's kind of quiet."

Annette pondered this new information. Remembering when she had first seen the boy in the post office, wearing his green Air Force parka, faded blue jeans, and carrying a heavy backpack, she realized that he probably was homeless. But he had seemed so naive. She recalled that he had asked for mail sent by General Delivery. What kind of mail was he expecting? How did he eat? Sleep? Stay warm?

"The bell's gonna ring in a minute." Pete interrupted her train of thought. "I'll see you later in the auditorium."

"Okay, Pete." Annette smiled, then gathered up everything she would need and closed the locker door. She watched as the farm boy she liked walked on down the hall, wiping his nose.

A couple of hours later, Annette followed the line of kids entering the auditorium. Chairs had been set up in front of the stage, which was decorated with twinkling red, blue, green and gold Christmas lights. The dark green curtain had garlands of gold and silver strung across the top, in swoops, and a large Christmas evergreen tree had been set up off to the side, glowing with lights and decorated with different colored ornaments which included colored glass balls, glittering icicle streamers, candy canes, miniature angels, elves and drummer boys. On top of the tree was a glowing yellow star.

Annette wanted to sit close to the front, if she could. The rows were filling up fast. Everyone was excited about the pageant. A few of her friends called to her, but she merely waved and made her way up until her eyes caught sight of Pete, standing in the front row, looking around for her. When he saw her, he grinned and beckoned her over, where he had saved a seat for her.

Mr. Edwards, the assistant principal, dressed in his dark gray suit coat, pants and tie, walked up on the stage in front of the curtain and held up both arms to make everyone grow quiet. Soon, with everyone seated, the chatting in the auditorium ceased. Mr. Edwards gave a short introduction, then left the stage.

Piano music began with the familiar melody of *Santa Claus is Coming to Town*. Then the curtains parted and the stage lit up, revealing a backdrop of a country scene with snow-covered hills, evergreens, and an artist's depiction of Santa's house at the North Pole. The scenery had been painted by students in the Art Department with reindeer on the front lawn and a sleigh parked in front of Santa's barn.

The choir was seated in chairs off to the left of the stage. There were about fifteen choir members ranging from freshmen to seniors. Penny, dressed in her white skirt and sweater, played the piano, off to the right, facing the center of the stage and the director.

The choir began singing, to the direction of Miss Barnes, the music teacher, who stood in front of them, her back to the audience. As soon as the first song was over, she turned to face the audience, which immediately fell into applause. Annette glanced over at Penny, who had peeked around at all the people in the auditorium.

Annette waved to her friend. Penny saw her and grinned. Then, at the direction of the choir teacher, Penny adjusted her music and got ready for the next number.

The choir performed two more songs, to which Penny accompanied them on the piano with grace and expertise. Annette felt Pete reach slowly for her hand and she let him hold it. Glancing up at him sideways, she saw his gaze was focused on Penny at the piano.

After *Sleigh Ride*, Pete — clapping loudly — turned to face Annette. "She's fantastic."

"Isn't she?" Annette grinned, clapping just as hard. She didn't listen to Penny's piano playing often enough. She was really quite amazed at how well her friend could perform. She knew that Penny had taken piano lessons since first grade.

The pageant went into the next phase — a dance performance by two senior girls, who did a modern dance interpretation to music from *The Nutcracker Suite*. This time there was a recording of Tchaikovsky music while Penny sat silently at the piano. The girls were very good, and got a lot of applause after they finished.

The choir sang a couple more songs, to which Penny played perfectly once again. Pete held Annette's hand the whole time, except when they had to clap. The choir sang *The Twelve Days of Christmas* and *We Wish You a Merry Christmas.*

The climax of the pageant came next. Four people from the Drama Club, dressed in costumes, acted out a skit while a junior boy, who was well known in the school for winning in Debates, recited by memory Ogden Nash's Christmas poem, *What's the Because of Santa Claus.* It was hilarious.

The poem and skit lasted fifteen minutes, and the boy who played Saint Nick made everybody laugh with his antics. One of the girls in Annette's English class played the part of Baby Nicolette, Santa's spoiled little sister, and then there was a senior boy who played the part of the "Erudite Child Psychologist."

The audience roared with laughter at the funniest lines. Annette laughed so hard, tears rolled down her cheeks. Poor Pete was laughing so hard, he ended up coughing … and *coughing* … and he coughed so hard that Annette patted him on the back.

"Pete, are you all right?"

Everyone was clapping and the actors were giving their bows. Pete whipped out his handkerchief and tried to make light of it. "I'm all right, Annette." He coughed again, then sat back in his seat.

"You're sweating," said Annette. It may have been bold of

her, but she reached her hand up to feel his forehead and drew it back right away. "I think you have a fever."

"Aw... I'll be okay." He turned his attention back to the stage. "Look ... Penny's gonna play again." He grinned, then wiped his nose with the handkerchief as the auditorium settled down.

The lights on stage dimmed, and then Miss Barnes, the choir director, invited everyone to sing along in the final number ... *Silent Night, Holy Night.* Everyone in the audience got to their feet as Penny began to play the introduction. Then the lights dimmed in the whole auditorium. Pete once again timidly reached for Annette's hand and she realized it felt cold. But she was happy just to be holding his hand.

When the pageant was over, Miss Barnes had Penny take a bow. Annette could see that her friend was red with embarrassment, especially when Steve Newton and a couple of his friends yelled out loud, "Way to go, Penelope!" Annette knew her friend hated to be called that. But she knew they didn't mean to hurt her feelings.

When they were out in the hall and school was over, Pete wiped his forehead and said to Annette, "I know I should have stayed home and rested this afternoon, but I really wanted to come and see the show." He walked Annette to her locker.

"Annette!" Tim came running down the hall. "Hey, Pete," he added.

"Hi, Tim. Your sister was terrific."

Tim smiled. "Yeah, she knows ..." He chuckled.

"No, she really *was*," insisted Pete. "I never knew she could play the piano like that."

Startled, Tim studied Pete. "Hey, you don't look so good."

As if in response, Pete burst out coughing again.

Annette said to Tim, "Can we get a ride home with you? I think Pete is still sick."

"Why, sure," said Tim. "I wanted to talk to you anyway."

He patted her arm, then said he would meet them out at the car in a few minutes.

"Dang … I'm really not feeling so great now," said Pete.

"Just wait a minute, Pete," said Annette. "I'll help you." She grabbed her coat and her things, and just then Penny showed up, beaming with happiness.

"Penny, I really thought you did a great job," said Pete.

"Why, thank you, Pete!" Penny turned to Annette. "What do you say we catch a ride home with Tim?"

"He's already said we could," Annette explained. "And Pete's sick, so we're taking him home."

Penny looked stricken. "Oh, *no!* Pete … are you okay?" She looked so worried that Annette was startled to see Pete transform into some kind of a prince, all of a sudden.

"I'm perfectly *fine,*" he insisted, standing up straight.

"No, you're not," said Annette and winked at Penny. "Come on, Pete." She started to help him along, but he brushed her off.

"I'm okay. Really." He cleared his throat.

"I have to go get my music and stuff," said Penny. "I'll meet you two out at Tim's car." Penny grabbed her coat out of the locker, then ran back down the hall as Annette led Pete toward the sophomore boys' lockers. He started coughing and moaning once again.

Minutes later, when they were seated in the back seat of Tim's car, Pete settled back and closed his eyes.

"Maybe we need to take you to see Mom at the hospital," Annette suggested.

"No, don't …" Pete sniffled, then reached for his handkerchief, which was starting to get really wet and gross.

The front passenger door opened just then and Penny fell into the seat. She swung around. "Tim's coming." She grinned at Annette. "Well, what did you think of the pageant?"

The girls rehashed the whole affair and compared their

opinions. Annette's favorite part had been the Ogden Nash skit. Pete continued to wallow in misery beside her. Finally, Tim got into the driver's seat and started up the engine.

While the motor was warming up, Tim turned to Annette. "I found out who that guy is you were asking about," he said.

"You mean, the hippie-looking guy with the greasy long hair?"

"Yeah. His name is Stu."

"Last name?"

"Nope."

"Stu?" Annette wrinkled up her face. "Stu ... Stu ... somehow that rings a bell. Where have I heard that before?" She looked at Penny, who shrugged.

"Well, what's he doing hanging out here?" asked Annette.

"Somebody said he's selling pot to kids."

"Whoa ..." said Penny. "*Really?*"

"Hard to tell," said Tim. "Could be just a rumor, you know."

Pete started coughing again, so Tim revved the accelerator. "I guess we'd better get this guy home."

"I'm okay," fibbed Pete.

Annette was still pondering the name Stu. She knew she had heard someone call somebody that name recently. She was so busy struggling to remember that she didn't catch the look that was exchanged between the boy next to her in the back seat of Tim's car ... and Tim's *sister*.

9

A Heart-to-Heart Talk

When Annette arrived home, Tim and Penny waited in the car with the motor running while she ran to the barn to check on Alice. Ginger had jumped off the back porch to greet her. The collie followed her inside the barn, where everything looked normal. Alice didn't show any signs of labor yet. Relieved, Annette ran back out to Tim's car and reported that all was well.

"See you in the morning," Penny told her.

Annette made her way to the empty farmhouse, glad that Penny still wanted to go on the walk and explore the old tower. It would take them an hour to get there, she figured. At least there wasn't any snow in the forecast for the weekend. But it certainly was cold enough. She went into the house and changed clothes, drank a glass of milk, then went back outside to do her chores.

Ruby sat in the comfy chair in Uncle Will's tiny living room, sucking on a red Tootsie Roll pop while she read a book she'd taken down off her uncle's bookcase. This one was about how to survive in the wild and gave all kinds of tips for camping and finding things in the woods to eat. Uncle Will was on the telephone, which was erected on the kitchen wall next to the icebox and the small, two-burner gas stove. She knew he was talking to somebody official. She tried to listen to every word.

"Yes, I'm concerned as much as you are," Uncle Will said into the receiver. "I just can't imagine why he would do such a thing. Believe me, it is not in his nature ..." After a pause, he said, "Ruth and Bob raised those kids right. My sister ... well, she had her problems, that's for sure. She drank ..."

Ruby knew Uncle Will was talking about her mother, Ruth Foley. She swallowed as a lump of pain mushroomed in her throat. Her eyes began to well up. Mom had been gone less than a month.

"No, I've told you ... I haven't seen my sister in years," said Uncle Will. "And if my nephew is running from the law, then there just has to be a mistake. I can't imagine him being in any sort of trouble."

But Ruby knew.

Uncle Will only knew what they had told him. Terry had brought her to Madison, all the way from Colorado, in order for her to be safe. Uncle Will was their only living relative, and somehow Terry trusted him. He made Uncle Will swear not to tell anyone where he was going.

When Uncle Will hung up the phone a minute later, he wiped his forehead with his handkerchief and filled a smudged glass with water from the sink's tap. "Little darlin', I don't know how much longer I can keep this up."

Ruby put the book on the little square coffee table and blinked at him. "Uncle Will, who was it? Who were you talking to?"

He drained his glass, then set it on the counter and turned to face her. He looked nervous. "The police ... actually, the FBI ... have tracked the two of you here, to Madison." He sighed. "They think you are here. They probably suspect that I am harboring a criminal." He shook his head.

"Will they come here?" Ruby was immediately afraid. "Uncle Will, they can't find me. They'll take me back to Colorado! You can't let that happen."

"How can I stop them?" Uncle Will looked at her with a frown. "I understand why you don't want to go back home. But surely the authorities will listen to you, Ruby. "

"They *won't* believe me," the girl insisted. "They think I made it all up."

"Well, they're certainly not going to put you back with the same foster parents," said her uncle.

"No!" cried Ruby, starting to sob. "How can they? Terry … he … he…" She burst into tears. Then she ran into the small bathroom, shut the door and sobbed, more for Terry than for herself.

Terry had called her last night. She had told Uncle Will, so it wasn't a secret. She was happy that her brother had found a place to work and was safe and warm in someone's house. She was terrified when he told her he'd had to "camp out" in the cold for a few nights. "When you see Uncle Will, tell him thanks for sending the money."

Now Ruby was afraid Uncle Will would tell the police. She knew he was afraid because of his job. If they found out he was keeping information from the FBI, they might fire Uncle Will. She knew he loved his job.

He had worked for the State Parks all of his adult life. Since she had gotten to know her uncle in the last week, he didn't seem so strange anymore. He had been kind to her and concerned only about her welfare.

She sniffed, thinking of her new friend Stephanie, who lived in one of the trailers in the mobile park. Stephanie was her age. They had become friends and Ruby had spent some time over at her new friend's home, watching television and listening to records. She had obeyed Terry's and Uncle Will's instructions carefully — not revealing anything about her past. When pressed, she had given the story that her parents were dead — which was true — and that she had come to live with Uncle Will, because he was all she had.

She wasn't allowed to tell anyone where she'd come from, or what had happened to her. It upset her to think about it. All that mattered was what was happening to her now. But she wanted — more than anything — for her brother Terry to come back. She didn't know what would happen next, but as long as the two of them were together, she felt safe.

There was a knock on the bathroom door. Ruby blew her nose. "Yes?" she called out.

Uncle Will said in a calm voice, "I made you a grilled cheese. Come on out, Ruby. Don't you want to watch *The Man From U.N.C.L.E.?*"

Ruby brushed her long blond hair, then went out to eat her supper and spend the evening with her uncle in front of his TV.

Penny and The Cheeze showed up at the Vetters' house promptly at eleven o'clock Saturday morning. The sun was shining and there was a clear blue sky. Annette had bundled up in her warmest winter coat with snow pants, heavy boots, and a long scarf for her head and neck. She let Ginger out the door and he romped in the snow with his playful young sheepdog friend.

"Good morning, Penny," called Mrs. Vetter, who was seated at the kitchen table, reading the morning paper and sipping a cup of black coffee. She hadn't been up long.

"Hi, Mrs. Vetter." Penny readjusted her stocking hat as she waited for Annette to finish putting on her mittens.

"Want to tell me where you girls are heading?" asked Annette's mom.

"Just over to Tower Drive," said Annette.

"That far?" Mrs. Vetter turned to look at them.

"Why not?"

Penny grinned. "We really need the exercise."

Mrs. Vetter took a sip from her coffee cup. "At least it's clear. I hope you don't stay out too long in this cold."

"We won't, Mom," said Annette. "See you later."

She pulled the door shut, then let the screen door slam as she followed Penny down the porch steps. With the dogs, they headed toward the end of the driveway, past the parked car, and turned right toward their destination.

It wasn't really any different from their short walk to the bus stop at the junction of Ogden Road and Tower Drive. But they would be going farther once they started walking east on Tower Drive, to the place where Tim had driven her and she had seen car tracks in the snow and broken tree branches.

"Is your mom doing better?" asked Penny. The dogs were up ahead of them, romping and checking out new smells along the side of the snow-packed road.

"I'm not sure," said Annette. "But this morning she seems a little cheerier."

"You told me you've been worried about her."

"I know." Annette sighed. "When she's depressed, *I* get depressed."

"But what do you think she's depressed about?" asked Penny.

Annette explained that she thought her mother was still feeling hurt over Earl Warner. "You know, when they broke it off after all that unpleasant land development nonsense, Earl said he'd call her. I think she was hoping he would."

"And he didn't, did he?" Penny sounded sad.

"Nope."

They walked a ways, and then Penny changed the subject. "You know, Annette, there's something I just have to get off my chest."

"What is it?" asked Annette. A car passed them from behind and she hollered for the dogs to stay close by them.

"It's about Pete," said Penny.

Startled, Annette smiled at her friend. "Yeah?"

Penny's expression grew serious. "I'm afraid ... Actually, I believe ... oh, Annette, I just don't know how to break this to you."

"Penny!"

"Pete *likes* me."

Annette kept walking. Penny's bluntness took her by surprise, but she wasn't really upset. "Oh, yeah?"

Penny sighed in despair. "Well, it's obvious. He's always looking at me. And yesterday, after the pageant, Pete just kept complimenting me."

"Well, Pen, just because somebody compliments you ..."

"No, it's more than that," she confessed. "For some time now I've been noticing it. Pete's *your* boyfriend, I know. I would never, *ever* try to come between the two of you. You *do* know that, don't you?"

A forced laugh erupted in Annette's throat. "Of course."

"And you're not mad?"

Annette looked right at her friend. "Penny, no. I'm not mad. Not at you. And not at Pete."

"But ..." Penny looked worried. "But ... you see, I don't really like him. I know he likes you, Annette, but ... but he's been dropping hints. It's just so ... so *queer*."

"No, it's not, Penny," said Annette. "Please don't worry about it."

"But, Annette ... I'm your best friend."

"Yes, you are."

"And I won't lie to you ... ever. Do you believe me when I tell you I'm not interested in him?"

"Hey, Pen, this may come as a surprise to you," said Annette, "but do you remember when Pete's cousin Luke was here in October?"

"How could I forget *that?*" Penny giggled. "Boy, Luke sure had the hots for you."

"All I'm saying," said Annette, "is that you can like more than one person. Pete and I are not engaged, you know. We're not even going steady, for that matter."

Penny laughed. "Oh, Annette, I'm so relieved. I was afraid you'd be mad at me."

"Well, I'm not, Pen."

They walked on a ways, and then Penny said, "Even if I *did* like Pete ... just a little ... what then?"

"There are plenty of fish in the sea," quoted Annette. "I am absolutely *not* mad at you."

"Okay," said Penny. "But I'd like it if we can change the subject now."

"Fine with me," said Annette. She listened to Penny's chatter as she talked about some of the kids she had gotten to know better from the Christmas pageant, including Scott Kowalski, Lisa's brother. But Annette was focused on her own thoughts as they churned through her head.

She was surprised that she hadn't noticed Pete's attraction to her best friend. A month or so ago, she would have felt devastated and betrayed. But strangely, now she didn't. Not in the least. When Luke had asked her to the Homecoming dance because Pete had been too bashful, Annette had become very attracted to the college-age nephew of Mrs. Randt. She had liked Pete again after Luke left, but then during the Thanksgiving weekend with the poachers and the Man with the Lantern, she had found herself attracted more to Penny's brother Tim.

Even that boy Terry, whom she'd seen at the post office and who was now working for the Randts, had left an impression on her. She assumed it was an attraction. He was quite good-looking, after all, and his manner was so different.

He was kind, helpful and had a familiar look in his eyes that made her question whether she had found a new attraction. She still felt excited whenever Tim was around, but nobody had to know about that—and especially not Penny. *Nope.* Tim would have to remain her own deep, personal secret.

The sun was at its highest point in the winter sky when the girls reached the pullout on Tower Drive with the path that went into the woods to the old abandoned tower. The tree line hid the sun and they were starting to feel cold. "This is where we go in," said Annette.

Penny looked around at the tire tracks in the snow and the scattered limbs and twigs. "Gee, it looks like someone was cutting firewood here, or something."

"You're right, Pen." Annette could see small piles of sawdust and a couple of fresh tree stumps not too far away. "Somebody was cutting wood here. I wonder who owns this property."

"I'm sure it's probably private," said Penny, "but there's no fence."

"There are no signs either," added Annette. "Maybe it belongs to the state, since the water tower is on this land."

"Well, we haven't been told to keep out," said Penny. "I say let's go see the tower."

The dogs took that as a signal to dash off into the woods on the small trail that cut between the trees. There were footprints both coming and going, along with deer tracks and those of small mammals and birds from the woods. The trail led about half a mile in from the road to the old tower, which was built in a clearing, on a small hill that had been cleared many decades ago.

Annette and Penny had always talked about going to explore the old tower, but just hadn't gotten around to it. Now they could see that it was very decrepit and looked dangerous to climb. It had been used many years ago as a water reservoir for the neighboring farmers. As they walked closer, following the tracks in the snow, they saw a structure on the other side of the tower.

"Hey, that looks like a shack of some kind," said Penny.

"A cabin of sorts," Annette guessed. "Let's check it out."

The girls hurried toward the building, which was not in good shape. It was more of a hut than anything else, with a sagging asphalt roof, a small window with a broken pane, and boards that were starting to deteriorate from wind and age. The dogs had already reached the building and were sniffing around on the south side, where they found an opening. There had once been a door, but it was gone. Instead, a large piece of canvas that hung from the opening served to keep out the cold.

"Somebody's been here," said Penny as they peered inside.

It was too dark to see and Annette was snow blind. She groped her way past the opening and stepped into the hut. It certainly wasn't any warmer than it was outside in the sun. "I smell charred wood," she said, waiting for her eyes to readjust.

"Look, there's a stove in here," said Penny.

The interior of the hut was no larger than the Vetters' chicken coop. As things began to come into focus, she saw the stove Penny had mentioned. A small cast iron potbelly stove was in the corner with a stack that curved through a hole in the wall to the outside. They could see the ash inside it and a pile of sticks and debris on the dirt floor beside it.

"Look," said Penny, pointing to the opposite corner. "It looks like somebody slept here."

Annette turned and saw an old ragged blanket scrunched up in the corner on top of an old torn mattress. Next to it were some empty food cans. She knelt down and picked up an empty can of pork and beans and two cans of Vienna sausages that had been consumed. "This explains the smoke Pete saw on the bus," she told Penny.

"Yeah, probably some hunter," said Penny. "Look, there's some orange peels."

"Most likely a poacher." Annette shivered at the thought.

"Let's hope not," replied Penny.

Ginger sat down at the hut's doorway and peered out from the canvas flap, panting after the long walk. The Cheeze sniffed around on the ragged blanket and then pawed it. Annette saw Penny's dog dig his nose underneath the blanket, his stub of a tail wagging.

"I think Cheeze has found something," said Penny.

Annette knelt down and felt around, then picked up the blanket. Underneath it was a small brown spiral notebook and a pencil. She reached for the notebook and took it over to the doorway, where she could read in the sunlight. Penny hurried over to look over Annette's shoulder.

Some pages had been ripped out, it appeared, but as Annette flipped through the book, a wallet-size photo fell out onto the ground. Penny stooped down to pick it up and held it in the light. It was a small school picture of a girl. She was young, about 12 or so, with blond hair in pigtails, wearing a red dress, with red bow ribbons on each pigtail. They stared at the girl's smiling face, and then Annette turned the photo around and they saw something written on the back, in pen.

Ruby 8th Grade

"Pretty girl," remarked Penny.

"Her name is Ruby," said Annette, turning it back so she could look more closely at the girl's face.

"I wonder who left this," said Penny.

Annette felt something else start to slip out of the notebook. "What's this?" She grabbed the folded-up piece of paper. It was a carbon copy from a money order. The amount was for forty dollars, and the money order was addressed to Terry Knutson, General Delivery, Ravensville, Wisconsin.

"He was *here*," said Annette. She turned to Penny, excited about the clue. "That new hired hand at the Randts' ... his name is Terry Knutson. Pete told me he was homeless."

"Oh, my gosh," exclaimed Penny. "That's awful. Imagine having to stay in this hut in the middle of December."

Annette looked more closely at the money order receipt. "There's a sender's address ... look, it says ... I can barely make it out ... it must have gotten wet ..."

"Let me see it." Penny grabbed the paper from Annette and studied it. "It says ... I think it says ... William ... William something ... it's hard to make out that last name ... but look here, it says Madison. The money order was sent from Madison."

Annette grabbed the receipt from Penny and looked closer. "You're right. It's from Madison, and it looks like the person who sent it was named William Knut... Knutson... William Knutson."

"The same last name!" Penny cried.

"He must be Terry's relative," said Annette. "Maybe his dad?"

"Why would he send the money, do you suppose?" asked Penny.

"I don't know. Maybe Terry's in some kind of trouble."

"And who's the little girl?" asked Penny.

Annette's mind was busy trying to put the puzzle together. She flipped through the rest of the notebook, but nothing else could give her a clue. The pages had been ripped out, so they looked around in the hut, in case any of the missing papers were there. They couldn't find anything else.

"We'd better start back," said Penny. "Are you going to take the stuff we found?"

"I don't know," said Annette. "I think we should leave them here." She pushed the notebook with the picture and receipt back inside, underneath the blanket. Then they left the hut. The dogs were already starting back toward the road through the woods, but Annette hesitated to look around once again outside the hut.

"I wonder what Terry's hiding," said Penny after they started for home. "I mean ... this is really a mystery, Annette. He shows up in Ravensville, like a homeless person ... but he has a dad in Madison ... and he's carrying around the picture of this little girl. It gives me the creeps."

"Oh, Penny!" Annette scolded her friend. "I'm sure it's nothing like that. Terry seemed really nice."

"Well, you only saw him a couple of times. How do you know what he's like? He might be a thief or ... or a kidnapper."

"Your imagination is running wild again," Annette taunted. But the situation had her worried. She prayed that Terry Knutson wasn't planning to rob the Randts. What if he had conned his way into working for them, only to steal from them? But that just didn't make sense. The Randts were poor. She knew they could hardly keep their farm in business.

Penny continued to make up scenarios as they trudged through the snow on their way back toward Tower Drive. The dogs were ahead of them, but then they took off into the woods after some varmint that caught their attention.

"Cheeze! Come back here," shouted Penny.

"It's all right," said Annette. "Let them go. They'll find us when we get to the road."

They walked on in silence. Soon they came to a driveway that veered off to the left.

"There's a lane down that way," said Penny. "I think it probably goes to a farmhouse."

"Maybe those people own this land," said Annette. Then, before they could discuss it further, they heard voices up ahead. Annette grabbed her friend's shoulder. Penny swung around. "What?"

"Somebody's in the woods," said Annette.

Penny listened. They could hear a woman's voice, but they couldn't hear what she was saying. Then they heard the voice of a man, who sounded a little angry.

"Are we trespassing?" Penny was alarmed. "Oh, Annette, what if they catch us?"

"Over here," said Annette, turning into the trees. She saw a large fallen evergreen tree they could hide behind if they crouched down. Penny followed her and they waited, trying not to move.

Soon a man and a woman, dressed in winter coats and boots, emerged on the snowy path from the road. They stopped before heading down the other trail. Annette almost gasped as she recognized the two. The man was tall and thin with long dark hair and a beard — the hippie they'd seen at Browns' Store named Stu. And the girl was heavyset — the redhead from the post office.

What were *they* doing here in these woods? Were they headed for the old tower, or the hut?

Suddenly, the couple stopped and faced each other. The man put his hands on his hips. "Maggie, we aren't leaving. I told you we're safe here."

The heavyset girl shook her frizzy red hair. "I don't feel safe anymore, Stu."

"Why not?" he growled.

"What about that kid who was here, cutting wood?"

"Aw, he was just some bum," said Stu.

"Well, I don't like the idea of him hanging out around here," said Maggie. "In fact, I think he maybe saw us."

"When?"

"You know … the other night … I told you I thought someone was outside the window."

"You're paranoid. You've been smoking too much of that Maui Wowie." Stu laughed.

"What if he was a DEA agent?"

Stu swore. "Come on, Maggie, get real."

"No, *you* get real, Stu. It's time to move on. This town is no good anymore. I thought things might cool down after Dave was busted. That kid might be spying on us. I saw him twice over at Browns' Store. And then there's that cop!"

"Brennan?" Stu's voice trailed off as the two of them turned and walked up the lane, through the woods, toward the farmhouse in the distance.

Annette stared at Penny and whispered, "They're talking about Bob Brennan."

Penny was shaking with fear. "Your detective friend at the police department."

"And something else..." Annette started shivering, too. "They mentioned Dave."

"Oh, my gosh," breathed Penny. "Dave Beck?"

"Yes," said Annette, "the drug dealer. And now I remember ... where I saw those two before."

"Where?"

Now that the coast was clear, the girls came out of their hiding place and started walking as fast as they could back to the road. The dogs had not emerged from their scampering in the woods yet, but Annette felt panicky and wanted to get safely to the road.

"Remember when we almost got caught in the back of Dave's camper? You know, when he drove out of our woods and didn't know we were inside?"

"Oh, my gosh!" exclaimed Penny. "*That* farmhouse! That's where he took us later when we ..."

"Only we escaped without him seeing us," Annette continued. "Those two people were there. And I remember now, their names were Stu and Maggie! Dave called them by name. I remember."

"Was that the house Luke drove you to on the night of the football game?" asked Penny.

"Yes," said Annette, recalling the adventure. "I asked him to take me there, so we could find out what was going on … and there was a party going on at the farmhouse. A bunch of hippies were there doing drugs. They thought we had come to join them. Luke and I barely escaped."

"Yes, I remember." Penny puffed as they hurried through the woods, plowing through the snowy path. Suddenly, the two dogs ran out of the woods and joined them, tongues dangling and tails wagging.

"And do you also remember …" Annette panted, "… when the police went to check out the house, Officer Murdock, who was new on the force and was paid off by Dave Beck … he said no one was there, just an elderly couple who had been sleeping."

"Well, we need to report this," said Penny.

"We will," promised Annette. "But we have to be careful."

"What do you mean, Annette?"

"Terry …"

"What about him?" asked Penny.

Annette turned to her friend. "What if he's involved?"

"You mean with the drugs?"

Then Annette shook her head. "The way they talked about him, I really don't think he is, though. But we need to find out what Terry is doing in Ravensville."

"Okay, you're right." Penny wiped her nose with her mitten. "But I think you should still call Detective Brennan."

"Good idea." Annette could see the road ahead of them now. She didn't see the hippie couple's blue Jeep, so perhaps they had just been out for a walk. The driveway to that farmhouse, she remembered, was down a side road that connected to Gaston Road, not far from the Randts'.

When she and Penny had escaped out the back of Dave's camper that day, they had found their way to Pete's house, where Annette and Penny had gotten a ride home from Luke.

Memories flooded her head from all that trouble with Dave Beck and his drug dealer friends. She did not want to go through that kind of trouble again.

10

Checking Alice's Condition

When Annette got home, it was getting close to milking time. She took off her coat and hung up her snow pants, which had gotten damp after their long walk. She could hear her mother in the dining room, talking on the telephone.

Ginger was waiting to be fed, so she got out his food and took care of that chore. She had decided to give the Ravensville Police Department a call and talk to the detective, Bob Brennan. But her mom was enjoying a long conversation with somebody. Annette walked in and listened.

"Well, unfortunately I'm scheduled to work the whole week of Christmas and New Year's," Mrs. Vetter said into the phone. "There were so many people at work who wanted the time off, and since it's just Annette here with me ..." She sighed, then said, "Plus we have a cow ready to give birth." She laughed. "That's right. Annette is so excited."

There was a long pause, so Annette swung into one of the dining room chairs and her mother turned and gave her a quick smile.

"Oh, he is?" Her mother chuckled. After a long pause, she said, "This really isn't the best time of year to travel. I'm sure Annette and I will make it up there to see you in the spring. It would be fun to go to the lake then. Yes, we'd love that."

Finally, Mrs. Vetter ended the call with, "Merry Christmas to you, too, Marie. Tell Joe I send my love." Then, after the goodbyes, she hung up and turned to face Annette with a heavy sigh. "That was your Aunt Marie."

"I thought so," said Annette.

"I'm just not up to driving to Minocqua for Christmas this year." Mrs. Vetter stood up and stretched. "How was your walk?"

"I'm tired." Annette yawned.

"Did you feed Ginger?"

"Yes, Mom. I'm going out to milk Elizabeth. But first, I want to call Detective Brennan."

"Detective Brennan? Why? Is something wrong?"

"No, Mom." Annette reached for the telephone. "I just had a question to ask him."

"Well, okay, dear." Mrs. Vetter picked up an empty glass from the table and carried it into the kitchen while Annette dialed the number to the Ravensville Police.

"Police department," a woman's voice answered after two rings.

"Hello," said Annette into the phone. "Is Detective Brennan there?"

"No, ma'am. Officer Brennan is off this weekend. He'll be back on Monday, though."

"Oh," said Annette.

"Would you like to leave a message for him?"

"Yes, please." Annette left her name and number with the dispatcher. She wasn't too concerned. It was not an urgent matter ... at least not yet. She only wanted to ask him his opinion of what she and Penny had overheard in the woods between Maggie and Stu.

While she was out in the barn, milking Elizabeth, Annette thought over the events of the afternoon and the notebook and the photograph they had found in the hut by the old tower. She needed to find a way to talk to Terry Knutson. But how? If she called over to the Randts', what would she say? No, she needed to talk to Terry, face to face, and see what his reactions would be.

Then she mulled over Penny's concern about Pete and how he had been looking at her in a new light. She had not wanted to let on that the news had taken her by surprise. Why hadn't she noticed that Pete liked Penny? Now that she thought more about it, he *had* paid a lot of attention to her, especially during the performance yesterday afternoon at school. Did this mean that Pete Randt was losing interest in Annette? And if it was true, and he was … why wasn't she devastated? Why didn't she feel a little jealous over her best friend?

Just then, Annette heard the barn door creak open. She turned her head as she continued milking and saw Tim walking toward her with his winter jacket on and a smile on his face. Right away, her pulse raced and she felt a flush creep over her cheeks. "Hello, Tim," she called out.

"I came by to check on Alice," he said.

"Good."

Tim walked over to the other cow's stall and felt her belly.

"How is she?" asked Annette.

"Aw … it's not time yet," said Tim.

Annette finished up and put the milk away in the cooler. "Are you done with milking already?" she asked Tim.

"We got done early tonight," said Tim.

"Hey, can I ask a favor?" Annette zipped up her coat as she stood in the doorway to the barn.

"Sure."

"Would you drive me over to the Randts'?"

"Oh, so you can see Pete?" asked Tim.

"Well …" Annette didn't know what to say. It was Terry

she wanted to talk to, not Pete. "Yeah," she finally said with a smile.

Tim shook his head and smiled. "What a caring little lady you are, Annette Vetter, to want to pay a sick call on old Pete."

Annette blushed. Was he mocking her? She didn't know what to say.

"Okay, I'll take you over," he said.

Annette had to go tell her mother she was leaving for a little while, so she hurried to the house while Tim waited in the Chevelle, warming it up for them. When she climbed into the front seat beside him, he gave her that warm look that always made her want to melt. Then he drove the car up toward Tower Drive and turned right in the direction of Gaston Road.

"Tim, there's something else," said Annette. "There's a farmhouse on one of these side roads behind the old tower. I want to drive past it."

"We won't be able to see much," said Tim. "It's getting dark out."

"I know, but I need to just see something." She didn't want to reveal what it was.

Without further question, Tim drove and Annette watched for the road. She wasn't sure exactly where it was anymore, but Tim turned into a narrow lane that went toward the woods around the tower. When he came to a farmhouse off the road, they slowed.

Annette could see lights on in the house and a Willys Jeep parked in front. It was too dark to see, but she thought for sure it was the same old green farmhouse that Dave Beck had driven to, and where she was quite sure his friends Stu and Maggie lived.

"Who lives here?" asked Tim.

"Stu ... and Maggie," replied Annette.

"Stu?" Tim had a puzzled look, then remembered. "Oh ... him. How do you know?"

Annette then explained to him how she and Penny had hidden in the woods when the two hippies had walked past them, headed toward the house on the path in the woods. "And I heard him call her Maggie," explained Annette. "Then I remembered that I'd seen them before ... when Dave Beck was at this house. If I'm right, those two are still here, and possibly dealing drugs."

"I thought the police closed up that drug ring," said Tim.

"Everyone did," said Annette, "but obviously not. That Officer Murdock was in on it, you know."

The porch light suddenly went on. "We're leaving," said Tim, and turned the Chevelle back down the road from where they had turned.

Annette did not protest. "I tried getting hold of Detective Brennan this afternoon," she explained, "but he's off this weekend."

"Gosh, Annette, did they harass you?"

"No, they never saw us," said Annette. "And the dogs were off chasing some animal when all this happened, so I don't think they knew we were around."

Tim drove up Gaston Road next, to the Randts' farmhouse. When he pulled into the driveway, they saw lights on in the barn. It was milking time on the Randt farm.

Both of them got out and went to the house. Right away, Billy Randt let them in, and all the kids ran in from the other room to greet Annette and Tim.

"I'm in here ..." called a male voice from the family room.

Kay said, "Pete's on the couch."

Annette could see Mrs. Randt and a couple of the girls in the kitchen, getting supper ready. Apparently, Mark and Mr. Randt—as well as Terry—were out in the barn. Pete was lying on the couch under a blanket with a pillow under his head. He grinned when he saw them, then coughed and reached for a glass of water on the end table.

"Hey, Pete, sorry you're sick," said Tim.

"I've got bronchitis," said Pete.

"Oh, no, that's terrible," said Annette.

"I should have stayed home from school yesterday."

"Did you see a doctor?" asked Tim.

"I'm on antibiotics," he said, "but I'll be okay."

"I was afraid you'd be out in the barn, working," fretted Annette.

"No. Dad has Mark and Terry to help him."

"Terry's in the barn?" asked Annette.

"Yup," said Pete.

"Do you mind if I go out there?" she asked.

"I don't think they need any more help, Annette."

"I just wanna say hi." She smiled. "Real quick. I'll be right back."

"Oh ... well, okay..." Pete looked puzzled. But Tim started talking to Pete about something else, which gave Annette the excuse to slip away.

"Are you staying for supper?" asked Addie.

"No, not tonight." Annette smiled at the 7-year-old.

She went out the door and hurried down the path to the barn. When she got there, she could see that Mark and Mr. Randt had just finished up the milking and were getting ready to go in and clean up before supper.

"Well, hello, Annette," said Mr. Randt. "This is a surprise."

"Come to see Pete?" Mark, who was 13, smiled at her.

Annette nodded. She noticed that Terry was in the equipment room. He didn't know that she was there. "Tim's talking to him," she said. "Is it okay if I talk to Terry?"

"Sure ... go ahead." Mr. Randt and Mark left the barn.

Annette wandered into the next room, where Terry was sweeping the floor, dressed in baggy jeans and one of Mr. Randt's heavy sweatshirts. "Terry?"

He looked up at her in surprise and froze, broom in hand.

Annette noticed that he had shaved off his whiskers, which made her pause momentarily. Finally, she asked, "Do you mind if I talk to you?" and moved toward him.

Terry's face relaxed and a slow smile spread across his face. He self-consciously brushed some of that blond hair off his forehead. "Annette ... right?"

"Yes," she said. For a moment they just stood and stared at one another. He was studying her face in a way that made her feel a little uncomfortable. She looked away, then sighed before meeting his stare once more. She wasn't sure how to approach him with her questions, but she needed answers. "This is awkward, I know. But ... but I just have to ask ... where are you from?"

After a long pause, he continued sweeping. "Why do you want to know?" he asked carefully.

"Well, don't you have any family?"

Terry stopped and looked at her strangely, thought a moment, then shook his head. "I did."

"You did, but not anymore?" She took it a step further. "What happened to your parents?"

Terry sniffed, then answered calmly, "They're both dead." He gulped.

"Oh, I'm so sorry," said Annette. She took a step closer. He didn't move away. "Well, if it's any consolation ... my dad died, too, when I was very young."

Terry just stared at her. He didn't say a word.

Annette's heart went out to him. "How about others? Have you got any brothers or sisters?"

"Do *you*?" he asked.

"Actually, no," she said.

"How old are you?" asked Terry.

"I'm 15. What about you?"

"I'll turn 17 in March," he said.

"Well, where were you born?" asked Annette.

Terry sighed, then started sweeping with the broom again. "I can't say."

"Well, why not? Is it a big secret?"

"Look ... I've got to finish up my work. If you'll excuse me..."

Annette wasn't about to give up yet. She decided to throw out a wild card. "Terry, I know you have a sister."

Startled, he frowned at her. "Who told you that?"

"Nobody," she replied.

He looked horrified for a moment, then relaxed. "I do have a sister," he finally admitted.

"And where is she?"

"I can't tell you," he said nervously. "Please ... don't ask any more questions."

"Why can't you tell me?" asked Annette. "What are you hiding?"

For the first time, Terry looked anxious and afraid. "Annette, please, just go. Who else knows about this? Who have you been talking to?" He was demanding.

"I ... I ... nobody. Honest!" He looked at her so hard, she was afraid. Annette backed up a couple of steps. "Were you staying out at the old water tower?" she finally asked.

Terry's mouth dropped open.

"Because," said Annette, suddenly needing to get it all out. "We went there today ... Penny and I ... and we found the hut where somebody had been staying. The reason we think it was you is because we found a notebook ... and a school picture of a girl named Ruby."

Terry stared down at the floor of the barn, looking defeated ... and terrified.

Annette continued. "We also found a money order receipt from somebody named William." For a moment, Annette was afraid he was going to lash out at her in anger. She knew she had taken a big chance revealing the clues she and Penny had found under the torn blanket in the hut at the old tower.

Finally, he leaned on the broom and let out a huge sigh. "All right. It was me. I did spend a coupl'a nights in the hut. Somebody I know told me there was an old ranger hut out by the tower that I could hi... *stay* in," he confessed. "But you saw how it was. Hardly a place to shelter in."

"I don't know how you managed," said Annette.

"Well, there was plenty of wood around," he told her. "I kept warm with the stove."

"I'm glad you came to work for the Randts," said Annette with a smile.

He didn't say anything. He was obviously very perturbed and nervous. He was no longer the calm and collected young man she had seen that first day in the post office, so confident and strong.

"Why are you here in Ravensville?" asked Annette.

Terry looked at her hard. "Pete said you were some kind of private eye. Well, I think you should be more careful about who you question from now on. And I've said enough."

"Okay," said Annette, "but I don't understand why you can't be up front with me. Unless, of course, you've got something to hide."

"I have a sister. So what?" Terry started sweeping with fervor. He was getting worked up now.

"Are you running away from something?" asked Annette. "The law maybe?"

"Annette!" Tim called to her from the front of the barn.

She turned around. "Be right there, Tim." She smiled at Terry. "Please don't be angry at me. I don't believe for one second that you are running from the police, or that you have done anything wrong, Terry. I just want to ... to get to know you."

Their eyes met, and even though Terry was still shaken by the line of questioning, his blue eyes softened and he managed a half-smile for her. "I'm just like you," he said, "only looking for answers." Then he turned around and swept strands of hay in a roll across the floor.

Annette scampered out of the room to meet Tim, who was waiting for her. "Everything all right in here?" he asked.

"Yes," said Annette. "Let's go."

On the ride back to her house, Annette started to cry.

"What's wrong?" asked Tim.

"Nothing," said Annette.

"What happened?" he pressed.

"Sometimes I'm just too darned nosy!" she cried, rubbing tears off her cold cheeks.

"Did that guy say something to you, Annette?" Tim's voice had become defensive and protective.

"No, it was my fault," she said, then sniffed.

"Sounds like you want to talk. Let's go into town and get a Coke."

"Thank you, Tim, but really ... I can't."

"Why not?" he asked.

"It's my mom's night off," she explained. "I want to spend some time with her. We hardly get to see each other anymore. She has to work a lot this coming week—including Christmas."

Tim dropped her off, then said he'd call tomorrow about Alice's condition. Annette hurried into the house, where her mother had supper waiting for her.

"Well, that was a long visit," said Mrs. Vetter. "Here, I'll dish you up some chili. How's Pete feeling?"

Annette suddenly realized how rude she must have appeared in front of Pete. She hadn't even gone back into the house to say goodbye. Reaching for the crackers, she said, "He's got bronchitis."

"Oh, that's too bad." Mrs. Vetter sat down at the table with her steaming bowl of chili.

"Mom, there's a boy staying at the Randts'," said Annette.

She crumbled a Saltine cracker on top of her chili. "I don't think I told you that I met him in town a week ago, when Lisa Kowalski and I took the Vietnam packages to be mailed."

"No, you didn't. What about him? What's his name?"

"Terry Knutson." Annette blew on her chili. It was still too hot to eat.

Mrs. Vetter had lifted her spoon, but held it in mid-air. Finally, she poked at some beans in her bowl. "What is he doing at the Randts'?"

"Mr. Randt gave him a job," said Annette. "He's homeless."

"Are you sure?"

"Well, that's what Pete said. And another thing, Mom … Penny and I discovered that Terry was staying out at the old water tower for a few nights."

"Good heavens," remarked Mrs. Vetter. "Certainly not *up* in the tower?"

"No, Mom. In the ranger hut. You know … the one next to the water tower. It's in pretty bad shape, but he stayed there. Penny and I found some things in that hut that belonged to him."

"I see." Mrs. Vetter tried a small spoonful of the chili, but made a face.

"Well, I'm afraid I started asking him too many questions," Annette resumed, stirring the contents of her bowl and submerging the cracker bits. "He … he got mad at me."

"What did you ask?"

"Just the usual … where he came from … if he had any family … and then I told him we found a photograph in the hut of a little blond girl. He admitted that it was his little sister."

Mrs. Vetter was silent. She had put her spoon down and waited for Annette to say more.

"I guess … he thought I was accusing him … of maybe … maybe running from the police." Then Annette's face collapsed and more tears burst forth. "I didn't mean to make him think that I thought that!"

Mrs. Vetter got up from the table. "I can't eat this right now." She picked up her bowl and set it on the counter.

"Mom, what's wrong?" Annette wiped her eyes. "Are you okay?"

"I'm fine." She sniffed.

"Is it something I said?" asked Annette.

Mrs. Vetter turned and gave Annette a stern look. "You and Penny must be more careful. One of these days, I'm afraid playing detective is going to get you into serious trouble."

"But, Mom ..."

Mrs. Vetter's look of disapproval upset Annette even more. "And I don't want to hear anything more about this boy ... this ... Terry Knutson!" She turned and stormed up the stairs to her bedroom.

Ginger, who was lying beneath the table at her feet, scrambled up to a sitting position and looked at Annette, then whined.

"Ginger, what did I say?" Annette felt terrible, all of a sudden. Then she pushed her bowl of chili toward the center of the table and buried her head in her arms for a good cry.

11

The Christmas Tree

"Uncle Will, are we going to have a Christmas tree?" Ruby asked. It was Sunday morning and she was eating her second bowl of Post Toasties with two heaping spoonfuls of sugar. All Uncle Will had in the trailer was powdered milk, so the sugar helped cover up the foul taste.

Her uncle had just gotten up a few minutes ago and was drinking his cup of instant coffee, seated in his comfy chair with the clothes hanging on the back. He scratched his head, then glanced over at her. "There's no room in this trailer for a tree, Ruby."

"Not even a small one?"

"No. Besides ... we're going to take a trip."

Ruby's eyebrows shot up. "A trip? Where?" She remembered how Terry had warned her not to go anywhere—and how important it was not to be out in public, where she might be *seen*.

"Up north," said Uncle Will. "I think we need to get away from here. The sooner the better."

"But where, Uncle Will?" asked Ruby.

"To Ravensville, to see your brother." He gave her a quick smile, then sipped from his mug.

"Really?" Ruby's face brightened.

"We'll spend Christmas in a cabin. How would you like that?"

"I'd love it," she said, lifting the bowl and drinking the last of the sugary milk-liquid. Then she wiped her mouth with the back of her hand. "Who does the cabin belong to? Will somebody be there with us?"

Uncle Will chuckled. "No. A friend of mine lets me stay in his cabin in the woods every once in a while. It's kind of rustic, but it's peaceful. We can ask Terry to join us."

"When are we leaving?" asked Ruby.

"This morning—as soon as we can," said Uncle Will. "I have to get a few things at the store, pack up a bag, and then we'll take off. Are you up for it?"

"Wait till I tell Stephanie." Ruby was excited after so many days being cooped up in this little trailer court. Of course, Uncle Will had taken her to the roller rink, and twice to the movie theater ... but he always went shopping by himself, and made it clear that she could be friends with Stephanie, but wasn't to talk to anyone else or disclose any facts about herself or her family.

"No, you can't tell Stephanie," warned Uncle Will. "You can't tell anyone where we're going."

Ruby hung her head. But she understood. It was for Terry's sake more than her own. "All right, Uncle Will."

"If you clean up those dishes, I'll get some stuff together." He stood up. "Then we'll be on our way."

Ruby could hardly wait. Not only was she finally going to get away from this depressing place, but soon she would be reunited with her brother. And Christmas was in just three days. She wondered if Terry knew she and Uncle Will were coming.

Annette was worried about her mother again. Last night, Mrs. Vetter had stayed up in her room and hadn't come downstairs until late. Annette had just started watching an old movie on TV, *White Christmas,* when her mother came into the living room dressed in her bathrobe.

"I love Bing Crosby," said Mrs. Vetter, who came and sat next to Annette on the sofa.

"It just started."

"Good." A moment later, she said, "Annette ... I'm sorry for the way I acted at supper."

"It's okay, Mom."

"No, it isn't." Mrs. Vetter settled back against a pillow. "I know I've been moody lately."

"Why? What's wrong, Mom?"

Mrs. Vetter sighed. "I have a lot on my mind."

"Well, maybe you should talk about it," suggested Annette. "Maybe it will help."

Mrs. Vetter patted Annette's leg. "I'll tell you when I'm ready."

They watched the movie, and during a commercial break, Annette asked, "When are we going to get our Christmas tree? Christmas is on Wednesday, you know."

"Oh, is it really?" Mrs. Vetter looked stunned. "I've been so busy, I guess I wasn't paying attention."

"We usually get our tree up at least a week before Christmas," Annette reminded her. "I guess I've been busy, too. And I've been waiting for Alice's calf to come."

"Did Tim check her today?"

"Yes. He said it wasn't time."

Mrs. Vetter sighed again. "Tell you what. Tomorrow morning, let's drive into town and get a tree and do a little shopping. I don't have to go into work until one."

"Okay." Annette brightened. "And, Mom ... that

Christmas Wish List I made ... you don't have to get me everything on it, you know."

"I wasn't planning to, dear." Mrs. Vetter made a face. "There were *some* things on that list not even Santa knows how to get."

"Like ... the horse?"

"The horse," said Mrs. Vetter, "and ... the *boy* ... with a good crop of hair!"

Annette blushed. "I was only messing around."

"I don't think you're going to have any trouble in that department," said Mrs. Vetter. "After all, there's Tim ... and there was that nice college boy, Luke Elliott ... and then there's Peter Randt."

At the mention of his name, Annette popped up from the sofa. "Oh, I forgot. I was gonna call Pete and apologize. But it's after nine o'clock. It's too late to call him."

"Apologize? For what?"

Annette explained how she had gone to the barn to speak to Terry, the hired hand, and hadn't gone back into the house to say goodbye to her boyfriend. "Oh, I can just imagine what he thinks of me."

"I wouldn't worry about it, Annette."

The movie had come back on. As they watched it, Annette kept thinking about what her mother had said about boys.

How did her mom know boys weren't going to be a problem in her life? She was still waiting for Pete to ask her out on a date. Homecoming aside, it did seem like he was losing interest in her, especially if Penny thought Pete liked *her* now.

And yes, there was Tim ... she had always been fond of Tim, always looked up to him, and now he seemed to be paying more attention to her, and no longer in the old "teasing" way that used to irritate her.

And there was still another boy ... Terry. Why did he interest her so much? What was it about that tall, blond, blue-eyed guy with the mysterious past?

The next morning, Annette was up early to do her chores. She milked Elizabeth and could see that Alice was not yet in labor. Just like Tim had said, Alice's udder was filling with colostrum, so she knew it wouldn't be long now till the calf was born.

After she fed the chickens and collected the eggs, Annette—with Ginger at her side—went to the house and found her mother ready to drive into town.

They visited all of the Ravensville stores on the main street. There were a lot of shoppers out on this Sunday, just two days before Christmas Eve. The stores were crowded and the clerks were busy.

Annette needed to pick out a gift for Penny and Tim, as well as something nice for her mother, and she also wanted to get a gift for Pete. But she didn't expect Pete to have to give *her* a gift. She knew how poor his family was. Then she thought about Terry. She wondered if she would have enough money left to get Terry a present too.

"Let's get the tree next," said Mrs. Vetter as they carried parcels to their parked car on the sidewalk. "It's going to be noon and I have to get home to get ready for work."

They found a smaller fir tree that they liked in the lot outside the Penney store. Annette helped her mother pull the tree on top of the roof of their sedan, and the teen-age boy working in the lot helped them tie it down with some twine.

"Hi, Annette."

Turning, Annette saw Lisa Kowalski on the sidewalk. With her were two of her younger sisters and a little brother, who looked to be 4 or 5 years of age. "Lisa, hello!"

"I see you've just bought your tree," said Lisa. "Hey, did you hear about the drug bust last night?"

"What drug bust?" asked Annette.

"My brother Scott told me some friends of his were downtown last night, and they saw the cops stop this guy who was speeding. Turns out he was high on something."

"Oh, my gosh." Annette wondered if it was Stu, the hippie.

"Anyway, he was a junior from Darwell Heights. Sounds like we still have a drug problem in Ravensville."

"It sure does sound like that," said Annette.

"Hey, I'm taking the kids over to Woolworths' for some fries and a cherry coke. Wanna join us?" asked Lisa.

Annette looked at her mother, who had just paid the Christmas tree lot salesman. "I'd like to, but my mom has to get to work."

Mrs. Vetter came over and smiled at the tall, dark-haired girl with glasses. "Hi, Lisa. How's your mother?"

"Just fine, Mrs. Vetter. Say, if you need to get to work, I could drive Annette home."

Annette brightened at the thought and shot a hopeful glance at her mother.

"If you have more shopping to do, Annette, I don't have any objection to Lisa giving you a ride home," said Mrs. Vetter.

"Oh, Mom, thanks," said Annette.

"Be good." Mrs. Vetter winked, then climbed into the car and slowly rolled down the street with the tree anchored tightly on top.

"Come on, everyone, let's go have lunch." Lisa led the way and Annette followed the Kowalskis as they crossed the street to the Woolworths' Drug Store. She had no doubt now that Dave Beck's contacts were still exploiting Ravensville with their illegal recreational drugs. The malicious drug dealer may be in prison, but his partners in crime were still out and about, and she made it a point that she would call Bob Brennan at the police department tomorrow morning.

An hour later, Annette was in the five-and-ten, searching

for a present for the last person on her list—Terry Knutson. She had decided that, even though she hardly knew him, she would get him something. If nothing else, it would show him she meant him no harm.

She had picked out a manicure set to give to Penny, and for Tim she had found some Brut aftershave. She bought Pete a pen light, and she had searched long and hard to find her mother's gift—a music box made of ceramic glass that resembled a piano and, when it was wound, played a tune to *You Are My Sunshine,* her mom's favorite song.

So far, she hadn't found the right gift for the Randts' hired hand. What did you get someone who is homeless? It would seem that they would need anything and everything. She didn't have much money left in her purse, so she had to choose carefully.

"Annette, the kids are ready to go home," Lisa called from across the aisle. Annette turned to see that the youngest Kowalski children were restless and starting to fight with each other. She knew she'd have to put this last present on hold, and followed Lisa and her siblings outside.

"I have to stop and get gas before I take you home," said Lisa.

"Oh, I'm sorry," said Annette. She knew that Lisa was going out of her way to take her home.

"No, it's all right, Annette." Lisa grinned and drove to a gas station on the highway.

"Jimmy works there," one of the Kowalski girls called out, and the kids laughed.

"Yeah, Jimmy's her boyfriend," piped up the little Kowalski boy.

Annette looked at Lisa, who blushed and said, "He is not."

"Oh yes, he is," taunted the other little sister.

A good-looking young guy, dressed in a uniform, with

dark, wavy brown hair and a mustache came up to Lisa's window. He grinned at her and she smiled back at him and said, "Fill it up, please."

"Regular or unleaded?"

"I don't care," said Lisa, obviously mesmerized by his presence. Annette stifled a giggle.

"I have to go potty," called out the young Kowalski boy.

"Oh, shoot," said Lisa.

"Stay here, I'll take him," Annette offered. She climbed out of the car and so did Lisa's little brother. A yellow station wagon pulled into the gas station right as Annette walked to the building with Lisa's brother. She noticed a blond man with a mustache in the driver's seat. Beside him was a girl.

"Want me to go in with you?" Annette asked.

"No, I can do it," insisted the little boy.

Annette waited inside the gas station, which had a few little items for sale on the counter, most of them hand-crafted Christmas ornaments. One of them was a little Christmas tree that glittered and had a bright red gemstone on top. There were other ornaments, apparently made by somebody's family member, because there was a placard that gave the name of the artist and penciled-in pricetags.

Suddenly, someone entered the station and Annette heard a doorknob rattle. Then she heard Lisa's little brother's voice shout, "*I'm* in here! Stay out!"

Annette spun around and saw a young teen-aged girl, who had tried to get into the restroom, which was locked. "He'll be out in a moment," she said and smiled at the girl, who had long blond hair and very blue eyes. Annette couldn't take her eyes off the girl.

"Oh, that's okay," said the girl, who immediately came to the counter, where the array of Christmas ornaments had caught her eye. She was drawn to them like a magnet as Annette continued to stare at her. Glancing out the big window of the gas station, Annette saw the driver of the yellow station wagon staring in and watching them.

"Aren't they pretty?" Annette said, reaching out to pick up an elf with eyes that were made of gemstones and a felt hat and jacket made of multi-colored yarn. "Somebody certainly is artistic."

The girl saw the Christmas tree ornament with the red stone on top. "Ohh... *this* one..."

"I know," said Annette. "I love that one."

The door opened and Jimmy, the gas station attendant, walked behind the counter to make change.

The blond girl fingered the red rock on top of the little tree. "I think it's a ruby," she breathed.

The attendant overheard and smiled over at her. "It's actually a rhinestone," he said. "My aunt made those ornaments. She uses stones for decoration. The gems aren't real, but they sure are pretty, aren't they?"

Annette studied the girl closer. She was quite certain this was the girl in the photograph she had seen at the old water tower — Terry's sister? *Could it be?*

"Ruby ..." murmured Annette.

The girl's eyes rolled toward Annette, as if she had called her by name. For a fleeting second, the girl looked frightened.

Annette immediately changed her tone. "I mean, the stone ... it's a ruby rhinestone."

"Well, I still like it," said Ruby.

Annette smiled. Right then, Lisa's little brother barged out of the restroom and announced, "I'm through. Let's go."

Ruby slowly put the Christmas tree ornament down, then turned and went into the restroom. All the while, Annette noticed the blond man out in the car, watching her closely.

"Come on, Annette," prodded Lisa's little brother.

"Just a minute. You go on out to the car. I'll be there in just a second."

Annette looked at the pricetag on the Christmas tree ornament, then opened her purse to see if she had enough money. Unfortunately, she was a few cents short.

After another minute, she walked out to the car and climbed in. Lisa was still flirting with the gas station attendant, but he had to finish waiting on the customer in the yellow station wagon.

As Lisa pulled out of the station and back onto the highway, Annette glanced out the window and saw the young girl, Ruby, run to the station wagon and climb in next to the blond man. She wondered about them. She might be wrong, but her gut told her she had just come face to face with Terry's sister and the man who might possibly be William.

12

A Startling Document

When Annette got home in the middle of the afternoon, she saw that her mother had managed to bring the Christmas tree into the living room, probably through the front door, which they hardly used. It was propped up against a corner of the living room, where Mrs. Vetter had cleared an area. But she hadn't had time to set it up in its stand.

Annette called Penny, who offered to come right over and help her decorate the tree. Half an hour later, Penny arrived and the two of them went upstairs to pull out the boxes from the storage room.

Mrs. Vetter's bedroom was at the east end of the house, close to the stairway. Her mother's room faced the road. Annette had one of the two bedrooms in the west wing, which looked out over the woods in back. There was a main bathroom on the second floor, close to her mother's room. The extra bedroom they used for storage or the rare guest.

"The Christmas ornaments and lights are in that closet that goes into the attic," said Annette.

"Gee, you've sure got a lot of junk up here," said Penny.

"Yeah, and there's more stuff in our attic."

"Well, don't get any ideas, Annette. It's too cold right now to explore your attic."

"There's nothing in there anyway," said Annette. "I've peeked in there more than a few times. Mom says we can't put anything of value in there or it will get ruined." She tried the pull cord to the closet light, but apparently the bulb was out. "Oh, great ... we're gonna need a flashlight, I think."

"I'll go get one," offered Penny.

"Look in the utility drawer in the kitchen," said Annette. She felt around in the dim light and lifted a few boxes out of the way. She had to move things around to get at the boxes she wanted. As she set a couple of file boxes up on the single bed of the guest room, she caught sight of a file folder sticking up that had recently been taken out and wasn't all the way pushed down. In the lamp light from the dresser, Annette saw a label on the file that read: THOMAS T. VETTER.

"My dad!" she exclaimed. Then, out of curiosity, she pulled the file folder out and sat on the end of the bed and opened the folder. There were a lot of legal papers in there, mostly things that had to do with her father's estate after he passed away in 1957. She had never seen any of these before.

She found a copy of the death certificate, which had all the necessary information and when he had died, where he had been born, what year, and so forth. Then she paged through the pile and found his birth certificate and also some papers in an envelope marked "College."

There wasn't much of interest, so she moved on and saw a group of photographs. She wondered why these weren't with their family album, which Mom kept downstairs on a bookshelf. She flipped through them quickly, but didn't recognize anyone in the photos. They were mostly from Dad's college days at Eau Claire. He hadn't met her mom until he had started working in the State Parks out of Black River Falls.

"What are you doing?" Penny had come into the room

with the flashlight.

"Oh, I found this box with some stuff that belonged to my dad," said Annette.

"Really?" Penny stood over her. "Annette, how cool ..."

"Yeah. I didn't know about this stuff." She pulled out another file that was marked "Annulment."

"What's that?" asked Penny.

Annette stared at the folder. "I don't know," she said, and opened the file. As she glanced over the documents, she saw her father's name listed and a date of August 31, 1951. Then her mouth dropped open. "This is strange," she told Penny.

"What? What is it, Annette?" Penny sat on the floor next to her.

"These are annulment papers for my dad."

"Are you sure?" Penny looked disturbed.

Annette's heart was beating faster. "He was married before."

"No! You're kidding."

Annette glanced over the document and saw that something had spilled and caused a big stain on one corner of the page. The ink had smeared and completely wiped out a portion of the paragraph.

"Pen, why didn't Mom tell me about this? I didn't know my dad was married to somebody else before he married my mom." Annette stared into her best friend's face, horrified.

"Well, who was he married to?" asked Penny.

Annette shrugged. "I can't make it out."

"Let me see that." Penny took the page, then handed it back to Annette. "It's too bad the document was damaged."

"It looks like coffee or something spilled over it," said Annette. The woman's name is no longer legible."

"Maybe there's more in that file," suggested Penny.

Annette slammed the file shut. "I don't wanna know."

"Well, when did your mom and dad get married? When

was their anniversary?" asked Penny.

Annette stuffed the file folder back into the box. She was confused. She didn't want to believe that her own mother had kept this information from her. What else had she not been told? "They ... my parents were married in June of 1952," said Annette.

"And you were born in August 1953," said Penny. "How old was your dad when he died?"

"He was twenty-nine, I think."

"Oh, Annette ..."

"I can't deal with this right now." Annette shoved the box aside and got to her feet. "I'll ask Mom about it tomorrow. Right now we've got some decorating to do."

They got out the boxes they needed. It took a couple of trips downstairs to get everything. Penny helped hold the tree in place while Annette screwed the trunk into the metal stand. Ginger lay in front of the front door, watching their every move.

Next, they unraveled the long string of Christmas lights and laid them across the carpet. Penny plugged them in, so they could replace the bulbs that were no longer working. Half an hour later, they had the lights on the Christmas tree and then began hanging the assortment of ornaments.

Penny asked Annette if she had talked to Detective Brennan at the police department about the hippie couple, Stu and Maggie.

"He wasn't working this weekend," said Annette, "but if he doesn't call me from the message I left him, I'll phone him in the morning." She then repeated what Lisa Kowalski had told her about the drug bust in town.

"That's so disgusting," said Penny. "After we helped catch Dave, I thought that would be the end of it ... with the drug problem in Ravensville, I mean."

Annette then told Penny about Tim driving her over to

the Randt farm. "On the way, I made him take me by that farmhouse where Dave drove us in his camper … where we saw Stu and Maggie for the first time." She then explained that they had left as soon as a porch light was turned on.

"And how was Pete?" asked Penny. "Is he feeling any better?"

Annette drew in a breath. "No, he's sick with bronchitis."

Penny gasped. "He shouldn't have come to school last Friday. Is he going to be all right?"

"He only came to school Friday afternoon, so he could watch *you* perform in the pageant," said Annette as she fixed a reindeer ornament that had lost its hook.

"Oh, Annette … I feel awful."

"Penny, it's not your fault." After a moment, she added, "Maybe it would help if you called Pete to see how he is."

"Me?" Penny looked dumbfounded. "But Annette, he's *your* boyfriend."

"I wouldn't say that," said Annette. "He seems to prefer you now."

Penny protested by erupting into a rage. "Annette Vetter! Bite your tongue! Anyone can see how crazy Pete is over *you*."

Annette almost retaliated with, "Then why hasn't he asked me out?" But she already knew the answer — Pete didn't have a car, nor did he get an allowance. Instead, she said, "We're just friends, Pen."

Penny stared, open-mouthed. "I can't believe what I'm hearing. Annette, you were crazy about Pete Randt when school started."

They worked in silence for a while, then Annette decided to change the subject. "Anyway, while I was over there, I talked to Terry, and he told me he has a sister."

"You didn't tell him about what we found, did you?" asked Penny.

"I kind of did," admitted Annette, "and he wasn't too

happy about it. But today I *saw* his sister."

Penny gasped. "What!"

Annette nodded. "In town. Lisa Kowalski stopped at the gas station on the highway, and while we were there, this yellow station wagon pulled in with a man and a girl inside. I'm positive that girl was Ruby, Terry's sister."

"Well, how do you know for sure?" Penny opened a package of silver tinsel to hang on the tree. "Did you talk to her or something?"

"As a matter of fact, we exchanged a few words," said Annette, and told about Ruby admiring the Christmas tree ornament in the gas station with its ruby rhinestone.

"That hardly is proof that she's the girl in that school photo," said Penny.

"Yeah, you're probably right," said Annette. "Most likely, I'm wrong." Then she asked, "What do you think we should do next?"

"About what?" asked Penny.

"The mystery. You know ... Terry. He is a mystery, all right." She sighed.

Penny laughed then. "Annette, do you have a crush on him?"

With a little squeal, Annette jerked up. "No, Pen."

"Well, I wouldn't blame you if you did." Penny giggled, then added, "Don't worry, I won't tell Pete."

"I want to find out what Terry's hiding," said Annette. "I know he's running from something ... or someone. I just don't know what ... or *who*."

"Where do you think he's from?" asked Penny.

"Well, Pete said he told them he was from out West."

"Out West? That could mean anything," said Penny.

Finally, the tree was all decorated. "Mom will be so pleased when she sees it," said Annette, stacking the empty boxes near the stairway to be taken up later. "Oh, gosh, it's starting to get dark. I need to milk the cows."

"And I need to get home," said Penny. "Hey, why don't you come over after your chores? My mom is fixing hamburger pie. You know you're always welcome."

"Thanks," said Annette, "but Mom left me a bunch of chili. I'm going to warm some of that up for supper. Then I've got some presents to wrap. What are you doing tomorrow?"

"Nothing," said Penny, getting her coat. "Come over and we'll play pool in the basement."

"Groovy," said Annette.

After Penny left, she and Ginger went out to put the chickens away, and then went to the barn to do the milking. Annette felt a little guilty because she had meant to check on Alice, the cow, before they got involved with Christmas decorations. Now she hoped Alice wasn't in trouble. She walked into the barn and was relieved to find both cows waiting patiently for her in their stalls.

That evening, Annette turned on the television and watched some Sunday night shows while she got out the gifts she had purchased that day and wrapped them up with Christmas paper they had left over from last year. The sit-coms all had Christmas themes that week. Then, because she was so tired after an afternoon of shopping and Christmas tree work, Annette went up to bed early and fell right to sleep.

The next morning, after coming in from chores, she glanced at the clock over the stove and wondered if it was too early to call Detective Brennan. She decided to wait a little longer, so made a pot of coffee for her mother, then grabbed some cereal out of the pantry. Ginger whined at her.

"Of course I didn't forget you," she told her dog, and ruffled his soft collie mane. She got out his food, and after he was fed, she sat at the table with her cereal and wondered how Pete was doing.

She still liked him. She couldn't deny it. But somehow he just didn't seem to be as exciting to her as he had in the beginning. She knew Penny cared for him, but Penny was too good of a friend to ever steal a boyfriend away. Penny still mooned over Steve Newton at school, who was too stuck up to like anyone but himself. But sometimes she thought Penny only feigned it. Annette had suspected for quite a while that Penny also liked Pete.

"And that's okay," she told herself, reaching for her glass of orange juice. "Isn't it, Ginger?"

The collie licked his chops and cocked his head at her, then barked a soft "yip" in reply.

"Well, hello, Annette." The friendly deep voice of Bob Brennan came over the telephone when she called the Ravensville Police Department half an hour later. "I got your message. What can I do for you today?"

"I might have some information for you," Annette said into the phone. "But first, I heard about that drug bust on Saturday night. Was that a local thing?"

Detective Brennan cleared his throat. "Yes, we did have an arrest, Annette. But we weren't able to get any information. Why? Do you know something about it?"

"Well, no, I don't really." Annette hesitated. "Penny and I were in the woods off Tower Drive on Saturday, and do you remember that farmhouse out by Tower Drive that I told you about?"

"What farmhouse was that, Annette?"

"Remember when that Officer Murdock brought Luke Elliott and me into the station on Homecoming weekend?"

"Oh! Murdock. Yes. Go on."

Annette sighed. "Some people were having a party back then, and they tried to get us to take drugs. Luke and I ran out of there and escaped. Then his car ran out of gas out on

Highway 10 ..."

"Yes, yes, I do remember that, Annette." Detective Brennan perked up. "Murdock went back out to check on it."

"And they had cleared out by then," Annette reminded the detective. "Dave Beck had come in and recognized us. That's when Luke and I got out of there fast ... and when the police went back to make an arrest, nobody was there ... except an elderly couple who had been sleeping ... or so he said."

"We know now, of course, that Murdock covered up the truth," said the detective. "The house is vacant as far as I know."

"Are you sure about that?" asked Annette.

"Not unless it got rented out. Tell me what you know, Annette. I've got a staff meeting in five minutes and I've got to get some reports ready. Can you cut to the chase?"

"Sure," said Annette. "When we were in the woods, we saw that same couple that was at that farmhouse back in October. Penny and I overheard them talking. We think maybe they're dealing."

"Do you know who they are?" asked Bob Brennan.

"All I know is their first names ... Maggie and Stu."

"Mm-hm." She could tell the detective was taking notes. "What else?"

"They said something about needing to leave town."

"Did they know you were listening?"

"No, we were hiding ... in the woods," said Annette. "I'm quite sure they didn't see us."

"And you think they're staying at that farmhouse?"

"Well, they took the path through the woods, over by the old water tower, that seems to go in the direction of that house. I can't be sure."

"Anything else?"

"No."

"Okay, Annette. Of course, you know there's not enough evidence for us to go make an arrest or anything. But I want you to do something for me, if you will."

Annette waited in anticipation. "Of course."

"I want you to stay away from there. Under no circumstances do I want you or your friends to go snooping around. We'll handle the investigation. But do report to me should anything more happen."

Disappointed only slightly, Annette thanked the detective and then they hung up. Then she turned to watch Mrs. Vetter come down the stairs, dressed in her bathrobe.

"What was that all about?" asked her mother.

"That was Detective Brennan," said Annette.

"When is he going to hire you?" Mrs. Vetter chuckled.

"Not anytime soon."

"The tree looks lovely." Mrs. Vetter poured herself a cup of black coffee. "You and Penny did a fabulous job."

"Thanks." Reminded of the ornaments and the boxes upstairs, Annette sat down with her mother at the kitchen table. "Mom, I've got a question."

Mrs. Vetter took her first sip and looked at Annette. "Okay?"

"Mom, was Dad married before?"

Mrs. Vetter's expression changed from calm to disbelief. "Annette, why would you ask that?"

"Mom, there was a file folder upstairs in a box. It happened to be sticking up a little, and I opened it and read some things about Dad. There were some *annulment* papers."

"Oh, Annette ..." Mrs. Vetter's voice faltered and her voice cracked. "Oh, *dear* ..."

"Why didn't you tell me?"

Mrs. Vetter took another two sips of coffee, then reached out her fingers and placed them on Annette's wrist. "Your father *was* married before. The reason I never told you was because it was such a mistake on his part. I didn't want you to think any less of your father, who was a very wonderful man."

"All right," said Annette, "so tell me ... what happened?"

"He met a girl in college," explained Mrs. Vetter. "It was long before he met me. This is what he told me. She was much too young for him and inexperienced. They had a whirlwind romance and he married her right after he finished his degree."

"And then what happened?"

"Well, she changed her mind. After a couple of months, she decided she no longer wanted to be married to him. So she got an annulment."

"Was Dad broken-hearted?"

"He told me it was a big mistake. They were totally wrong for each other. They fought all the time, plus she had a drinking problem. Finally, she went to a lawyer and had papers drawn up ... and that was that." She took another sip of the coffee.

Annette let that news soak in. "Who was this woman that he married? Do you know her name?"

"You didn't read that on the paper?" asked Mrs. Vetter.

"No," said Annette. "Someone had spilled something on the paper and I couldn't make out who it was." She sighed, then asked, "Maybe it's better if I don't know."

"Well, her name was Ruth," said Mrs. Vetter. "But she moved away from here. Your father never really gave it a second thought. That's the reason I never brought it up."

"Mom, I'm sorry," said Annette. "I didn't mean to bring up the past and make you feel bad."

Mrs. Vetter stood up and as she walked to the counter, Annette noticed her mother's hand was shaking. She dumped the rest of her cup into the sink, then headed for the stairs. "I'm going up to take a shower."

"Do you want me to make you anything to eat?"

"No, I'll be fine."

Annette suddenly felt that it was all her fault. Now she had caused her mother to be depressed again. Thinking about her deceased husband was sad enough around Christmas time, but now Annette had scared up a worse ghost ... her dad's first wife.

13

Some Afternoon Pool

The sun came in through the little round window in the loft. Ruby awoke on the bed next to the opposite wall and stared at the logs all around her. How comfortable the bed had been in this cabin, after having to sleep on Uncle Will's lumpy couch.

Pine scent and wood smoke coming from the fireplace downstairs filled her nostrils. She could hear the crackle of a fire. Uncle Will, she guessed, was already up and had built a fire to warm things up.

Ruby had been using one of her uncle's white undershirts for a nightgown, since she hadn't brought any extra clothes with her from Colorado. She stepped into some slippers he had bought her, then went across the room to get her pair of jeans and her flannel shirt – also one of Uncle Will's.

When she climbed down the ladder out of the loft, he was poking at the flames in the hearth.

"It's nice and cozy in here," said Ruby with a grin on her face.

"Yes, it warms up fast in here."

The cabin was bigger than his trailer, which wasn't saying much. It consisted of three rooms – the largest of which was the living area, which contained an eating table and kitchenette –

and there was a small bedroom off to the side, plus a small bathroom that had a tiny sink and a special toilet that used chemicals. Uncle Will called it the "porta potty."

"I slept like a baby up in that loft," said Ruby. "How did *you* sleep, Uncle Will?" He had slept downstairs on the roll-away bed.

"With my eyes closed," said Uncle Will. "I'll make some scrambled eggs for us in a little while."

"Is there a toaster?" asked Ruby, looking around.

"Nope. But you can toast some bread over the fire, if you want."

"Just like camping," said Ruby.

"Just like camping," he echoed.

"When will I get to see Terry?" she asked.

Uncle Will sighed. "I need to drive into town to call him. After breakfast I'm going. You can either come along or stay here."

"I'll stay here," Ruby decided.

"Fine," said Uncle Will.

"Whose cabin is this, anyway?" she asked. "I sure like it here."

"It's certainly rustic," said Uncle Will, "but it's warm and no one will find us. It belongs to Joe Tucker, one of the rangers I work with sometimes during the summers."

"Is it his home?"

"No, he uses it for vacations and hunting."

"He's lucky."

"But of course, there's no electricity or phones out here in the woods. At least he left us a pile of firewood."

Ruby walked over to the front window and looked into the snow-covered woods, then off to the side, where there were some rolling white hills and more forest. "Does Terry know we're here?" she asked.

Uncle Will put the poker back into the stand with the

other fireplace tools. He closed up the screen and settled back in a lawn chair covered with an army blanket. "I wasn't able to reach him last night," he told his niece. "I left a message for him at that farm where he's working, but I didn't have a phone number I could leave with them."

"But when you get hold of him, will you bring him here?"

Uncle Will smiled at her, but there was pity in his eyes. "I'm hoping the three of us can spend Christmas together ... in this cabin."

"Oh, Uncle Will, can we get a tree?" Ruby grew excited at the thought. "Can we cut one down?" She looked out the window, searching for prospective evergreens.

"Now, hold on a minute," he said. "We can't just start cutting down trees on Joe's property."

"When Dad was home last year at Christmas, we had a huge tree." Ruby sat in the other lawn chair beside Uncle Will. "It was my favorite Christmas. We had presents and cookies and a turkey ... and Grandma came over. Daddy had to go get her ... she was in a wheelchair then ... and Terry ... he ... he ..." A sob escaped and she turned her face away. "I'm sorry, Uncle Will."

"Ruby, you have every reason to cry," said Uncle Will.

"First, Grandma passed away." Ruby sniffed, struggling to control herself. "Then Daddy ..."

"We don't know about him," Uncle Will reminded her. "Your papa might still be found."

"Mama didn't think so. She ..." Ruby burst into tears once again. "Ohhh ... Christmas will never be the same!" She ran to the ladder and climbed quickly up to the loft, where she collapsed on her bed and buried her face in the pillow.

After lunch and Annette's mother had gone to work, Annette walked over to the Duncan farm with Ginger trotting alongside of her. The sun had disappeared before noon and clouds were gathering. Snow was predicted for the evening.

Penny was busy in the kitchen when she came through the front door into the Duncans' living room. "I'll be right out," she called to Annette.

"Hi, Annette," called out Karen, Penny's 6-year-old sister, who was paging through a Sears Roebuck catalog on the living room carpet.

"What are you doing, Karen?" Annette asked. Before she shut the door, she watched as Ginger and The Cheeze touched noses on the front porch, their tails wagging. Then the two dogs wandered off around the side of the house.

"I want Santa to bring me a bike," said Karen. She turned a page and pointed a stubby finger. "Like this one." Then she squealed with excitement. "Santa's coming tomorrow night!"

"I know," said Annette.

Penny walked out of the kitchen with a white linen dish towel hanging over her arm. "Come in here and taste this fudge."

"You made fudge?"

"My mom asked me to," said Penny. "I made both chocolate and peanut butter."

"Oooh ..." Annette followed her friend into the Duncans' kitchen, which was a mess with bowls and a double boiler and splotches of chocolate covering the stove and the counter top. She picked up a piece of fresh peanut butter fudge and stuck it in her mouth. "Mmm ... delicious."

"No calf yet?" asked Penny.

"Nope."

Penny sighed. "Well, I called Pete this morning."

"You did?"

"He's feeling better today."

"Oh, I'm so glad," said Annette. "I should give him a call, too."

"As soon as I put this stuff away, let's go downstairs and play some pool."

"Okay," said Annette. "I'll help you."

Fifteen minutes later, they had the dishes put away and the kitchen in order once again. Mrs. Duncan came upstairs from the basement with her laundry basket. "Well, hello, Annette. I hope you and your mother will be able to join us for Christmas dinner on Wednesday."

"I'm afraid Mom has to work on Christmas again this year," said Annette.

"Oh, that's too bad."

"Then you can take her some left-overs," said Penny. "Come on. Tim said he'd be in after he gets back. He went with Dad somewhere."

The Duncans had a pool table in their basement, which was one of their favorite activities. Penny turned on the radio while Annette got down her favorite pool cue and looked around for the chalk. Christmas carols played and Penny hummed along for a few seconds.

Annette told Penny about calling Detective Brennan that morning, and what he had said about Stu and Maggie. "He doesn't want us to go near them."

"Yeah, well, they'll probably leave before they get caught," said Penny.

Annette racked up the balls and Penny broke with her cue stick. While they were playing a game to warm up, Annette told her friend about the conversation she'd had with her mother that morning, about her father being married before.

"I can't believe she never said anything," said Annette.

"Sometimes people just don't like to talk about things like that," said Penny.

"Well, I think it's strange that that file folder was sticking up out of the box," said Annette. "I have a feeling my mom was going through it recently."

"Yes, but why?" asked Penny.

"I don't know, Pen. It's another mystery."

There were footsteps on the basement stairs and a moment later, Tim appeared with a grin on his face. "Hey, you two, who made the fudge?"

Annette pointed to Tim's sister.

"Why didn't you put nuts in it?" he complained.

"I don't like nuts in fudge," whined Penny. "They give me cankor sores!"

"Whah-*whah*..."

Annette giggled and then leaned over and took a shot, sending one of the balls into the far pocket.

"Dad and I just got back from town," said Tim. He selected his cue off the wall and reached for the chalk. "We had to go to the Farm and Fleet, and then we stopped to put some gas in the truck." He watched as Annette posed herself for another shot.

She missed and stepped aside for Penny.

"Anyway," resumed Tim, wiping the end of his stick with the chalk, "Bob Brennan was there and he had an FBI agent with him."

"An FBI agent?" Penny stood up before taking her turn.

"Yeah."

"At the Farm and Fleet?" asked Annette.

"No, the gas station," said Tim.

"What were they doing *there?*" she asked.

Penny took her shot and missed. "Oh, darn ..."

Tim wiped some dark strands of hair off his forehead. "Detective Brennan said they were looking for a missing girl. They put a flier up on the door of the gas station."

"A missing girl?" Annette's mind began to click.

"Yeah, somebody from Colorado."

"Ooh," said Penny, suddenly interested.

"The FBI agent said they think the girl ran away with her older brother."

"What?" Annette suddenly grew fearful. "Tim, tell me what he said. Please."

"Why?"

"What does the girl look like?" asked Penny.

"Well, it was a black-and-white photo of her face. She's about 13 or 14 years old and has blond hair. Her name is Ruby Foley."

Both Annette and Penny gasped at the same time and stared at each other.

"Do you know something?" Tim looked at them suspiciously.

Annette sighed with relief. "It can't be her," she said to them. "Terry's last name is Knutson."

"Terry? At the Randts'?" Tim looked alarmed.

"Yes," said Annette. "He has a sister named Ruby. We found her picture over at the water tower. He had some of his things in that hut, where he stayed until he went to work for the Randts."

"Maybe you'd better call Detective Brennan, Annette," said Penny.

Annette set her cue stick down. She turned to Tim. "Why do they think this girl is here? In Ravensville?"

"I don't know," said Tim. "Apparently they tracked her down somehow."

"Detective Brennan would know," said Penny. "Let's call him now."

"No," said Annette. "Not yet. First, I need to talk to Terry." She started for the stairway.

"Wait, where are you going?" asked Tim.

Annette stopped and faced them. "I'm going to call over to the Randts'. Can I use your phone?"

"I'll come with you," said Penny.

Both Penny and Tim followed Annette up the stairs, where she made the call to the Randt farm from the Duncans' living room. When she got through, Mrs. Randt was the one who answered the phone.

"Well, hello, Annette," said Mrs. Randt. "Pete's in the barn. I'm sorry you missed him."

"That's okay, Mrs. Randt," she said. "Can I talk to Terry?"

"Terry?" Mrs. Randt hesitated, then said, "Well, he's not here."

"Well, when he comes back, could you please have him call me? I'm at the Duncans'."

"No, I'm afraid he's left," said Mrs. Randt.

"What do you mean he's left?"

"He said he had to leave for a couple of days. Something to do with his family." Mrs. Randt covered the phone with her hand and Annette heard her yell at some kids to quiet down. When she came back on, she said, "Honestly, I don't know if he's coming back to work here. He seemed awful worried about something."

"Oh," said Annette, disappointed. "Well, okay."

"Do you want me to have Pete give you a call later?" asked Mrs. Randt.

"Uh ... sure," said Annette.

When she hung up, Tim and Penny were waiting to hear the news. Annette told them that Terry had left and may not be coming back.

"He *is* running from the law. I just knew it," said Penny.

"Cut that out," chided Tim. "What are you gonna do, Annette?"

"I don't know," she said.

"Well, there's not much we can do about any of this," said Tim. "Let's just go back downstairs and play some pool."

Annette didn't feel much like playing, but she swallowed and tried to put Terry's leaving out of her mind as she followed Penny and her big brother back down into the basement. They opened some bottles of pop and Tim put on some records, and soon the problem with Terry and his sister had moved to the back of her thoughts.

When it was time to go home and do the milking and her other chores, Annette's thoughts returned to Terry and his sister. Ginger trotted at her side as they hurried down the road. Snowflakes had started falling. It looked like a Christmas storm was moving in.

Ruby had built a snowman out in front of the cabin. When her uncle's yellow station wagon drove up the long, winding driveway, she shouted with glee, expecting her brother to be in the car. But he wasn't. Uncle Will climbed out with a worried face.

"Where's Terry?" Ruby asked. With her mitten, she rubbed the end of her nose.

"He left," said Uncle Will.

"Where did he go?"

"They don't know, Ruby."

"Who? Who doesn't know?"

"The people he was working for. They said he left this morning."

"But why? Did he do something wrong?"

"No, I don't think so, Ruby."

"Then what? Tell me, Uncle Will. Where is Terry? Aren't we gonna be together for Christmas?" She started to cry.

"Come on inside the cabin. I'll build up the fire."

Ruby continued to cry. She had known this was going to be her worst Christmas … *ever*.

Annette had just gotten off the phone with Pete as she put on her coat and scarf. It was time to go out and milk Elizabeth and check on Alice. The snow was swirling around now and adding to the snowpack that was already on the ground. While she sat and milked the cow, she contemplated all of the mixed-up thoughts going through her head.

She was concerned about Terry. Pete had told her what he knew, plus he had mentioned that Detective Brennan and the FBI agent, Mr. Chase, had been out to the farm that afternoon, asking about Terry.

"They wouldn't say why they were looking for him," Pete had told her. "We asked because we were worried he might have committed some crime."

"He can't be a criminal," Annette had told Pete.

"Are you sure about that?"

"Well, no," Annette had admitted. But in her heart she couldn't accept the possibility. She remembered the first time she had seen Terry, in line at the post office, confronting Maggie when she started voicing her disdain for the war in Vietnam.

"I'll call you if I find out anything," said Pete. Then they had said goodbye and hung up.

And her mom ... Annette was so worried about Mrs. Vetter. She was working too hard, for one thing. She had taken on extra hours ever since the breakup with Earl Warner. It was as if her mother needed something to fill her time, to fill the emptiness of not having a man in her life.

"*I'm* not enough," Annette mumbled to herself. "I never thought about it until now." She realized that she had been her mother's main concern ever since Annette's father had passed away in 1957. "And now I'm growing up ... I'm able to take care of myself, and I'm getting interested in boys ... and Mom ... oh, poor Mom ..."

A tear fell from Annette's eyelid and she sniffed. Elizabeth mooed and turned her head.

"I'm sorry, Lizzie." Annette finished the milking, then fed the cows and saw that Alice's condition was unchanged. The pregnant cow had a tired, sad look in her brown eyes. Annette patted the cow's forehead and said to her, "Everything's gonna be all right, Alice. Maybe you'll give us a Christmas present."

She put the milk away, then turned out the lights in the barn and closed up the chicken coop before going into the house. Ginger followed her in, and waited patiently for his kibble as she hung up her coat, scarf and mittens, which were wet from the snow.

After her dog was fed, Annette wandered into the living room and plugged in the Christmas tree lights. All of the colors really did make the room look beautiful. She had to admit, she and Penny had done a super job decorating the tree.

Annette was making herself a ham sandwich after cooking up a box of macaroni and cheese when there came a knock on the back door. Ginger leaped up from his spot under the kitchen table and barked, beating her to the door.

Flicking on the porch light, Annette peeked out the window and saw someone standing on the porch in a green jacket. Her heart skipped a beat. Then she opened the door and faced Terry Knutson.

14

An Overnight Guest

"Terry!" cried Annette. "What are you doing here?" "Annette," he said. "May I come in, please? It's really cold." He was shivering. She let him in and closed the door. "Is your mother here?" he asked.

"Why, no." Annette stared at him.

Terry hesitated, then said, "I ... I was hoping ... maybe I could stay in your barn tonight."

"Take your coat off," she told him. "Come on in and get warm."

"I'm sure you're wondering why I'm not at the Randts'," he said as he removed his parka and hung it on the hook behind the door, where Annette pointed.

"Terry, the FBI is looking for you," said Annette.

"Yes, I know. That's why I had to leave. I was going to go back to the tower and stay in that hut. But I figured ... that's the first place they'd look for me."

Annette continued to stare at him, baffled.

"I'm not gonna hurt you," Terry said in a soft voice. He tried to smile, but Annette could see that the boy was deeply troubled.

"Did you walk all the way in this snowstorm?" Annette

peeked out at the swirling flakes.

"I cut across some woods," he said as he removed his boots and set them under his wet parka.

"I was just going to have some macaroni and cheese," said Annette. "Would you like some?"

"I'm starved."

"And how about a ham sandwich? I'll make another one." Annette hurried to the refrigerator and got out what she needed while Ginger sniffed Terry's pants legs. A glance over her shoulder showed him squatting down and rubbing the collie's rich mane. Ginger's tail swished in friendship as he nosed the boy's chin.

"You have a beautiful dog," said Terry. "What's his name?"

"Ginger."

"Do you mind if I wash up?" Terry stood.

"Oh, of course!" Annette showed him the downstairs bathroom, then returned to her sandwich-making task. Excitement coursed through her veins. The last time she had spoken to Terry, he had been upset by her questions. *He must have been desperate to come here,* she thought. She was dying to hear what he had to say, and wondered how Penny would react when she told her friend Terry Knutson was in her house ... *wanted by the FBI.*

Annette poured each of them a glass of fresh milk and was setting the kitchen table when Terry came in from the bathroom. He seemed tired and stressed out as he pulled out a chair and sat down. Annette joined him and watched as he took a large bite of the sandwich. "Mm, good," he told her. She smiled, then began to eat hers.

"Something tells me I can trust you," Terry said halfway through the meal. "If I'm wrong, then just tell me now ... and I'll leave ... and never bother you again."

"Well ..." Annette blinked, then said, "just tell me the

whole story. Then I'll decide."

"Fair enough," said Terry. "After all, what do you know about me?"

Annette shrugged and reached for her glass of milk. "Okay, I'm listening."

Terry hung his head and dangled the fork over his plate with a macaroni noodle on the end of it. "Something happened the week of Thanksgiving," he said. "Back in Colorado Springs, where I was living with my mom and my sister Ruby."

"The girl in the picture," commented Annette, and Terry nodded.

"You see, our dad is … *was* … in the military. He got deployed to Vietnam about a year ago. He's been in the Air Force a long time. My mom met him after he came back from Korea." He lifted the fork and ate the dangling macaroni, then set the fork down and continued his story.

"About last June, we learned that the airplane Dad was in had gotten shot down close to Hanoi. There was no evidence that he'd died in the crash. I mean, his body wasn't found … so they had to list him as M.I.A."

Annette knew that meant Missing in Action. She felt so sorry for Terry and his family.

He went on. "There was no word about him for weeks and weeks. But then, right around Halloween, Mom got a letter from the Pentagon. Dad was in a P.O.W. camp. He was reportedly in very bad shape and they couldn't rescue him. The Air Force told us he wouldn't live much longer."

Annette released a moan and covered her mouth. "I'm so sorry …"

"There's more," said Terry and sat up straighter in his chair. "My mother was worried sick, of course, and she had a history of drinking. It got worse … much worse." He swallowed. "The week after Thanksgiving, Mom took her life. She was drinking heavily one night and she took a whole bottle of sleeping pills."

Annette was silent. She waited for Terry to continue.

"My sister and I didn't have any relatives there in Colorado. Our grandma—my mom's mom—was in a home after having a stroke, and she was in a wheelchair. Well, she passed away a couple of months ago. The only other relative we have is our mom's brother, Uncle Will, who lives in Madison."

Annette was thinking, *Ah-ha ... William Knutson ... Uncle Will.*

"Social Services came and said Ruby and I had to go to foster homes," said Terry. "That wouldn't have been so bad, really, except that they split us up. I didn't want that. I thought the two of us should stay together. But they put Ruby in with a retired Air Force couple. These people took in foster kids quite often. As for me, one of my friends from high school talked to his parents, and they let me live with them temporarily. I tried to talk them into taking Ruby too. I wanted her to be with me. But Charlie's mom worked and Social Services decided she needed a full-time foster mom, especially after the traumatic death of our mother."

"Were you able to visit your sister?" asked Annette.

"Well, it was across town, but my friend Charlie would drive me over to see Ruby." Terry took a drink of his milk, then said, "A coupl'a weeks ago, I decided to drop in without calling first ...even though I wasn't s'posed to do that. That's when I caught Colonel Yates molesting my sister." A dark look crossed Terry's face as he recalled what he had seen. "She was screaming and fighting him ... and when I walked in, I told him to stop."

"Gosh," breathed Annette. "Go on."

Terry looked at Annette, his lip trembling. "He wouldn't stop. He was hurting her. I had to do something ... so I attacked him. For an older guy, he sure knew how to fight. But I kept on him. Ruby managed to crawl away and hide behind a piece of furniture, and then he was coming at me again ... this time with a baseball bat which Mrs. Yates had in her hand. She came into the room after hearing all the ruckus, and she just stood there, watching. But I fought him. I managed to grab hold of a heavy vase ... and I *hit* him."

Annette couldn't move. She could hardly breathe, watching Terry's emotions as he relived the awful memory. She waited, and he went on.

"I knocked him out cold," said Terry. "Then Mrs. Yates stood there, screaming at me, saying she was going to call the police. Ruby was crying and sobbing and begging for me to take her away from there. I must have hurt Colonel Yates really hard on the head ... I think I might have bashed in his skull." He choked on that last word and buried his head in his hands.

"Oh, Terry," murmured Annette. She paused a moment, then asked, "So what happened next?"

Terry recovered and took a couple of breaths to compose himself. "Mrs. Yates kept yelling at me, saying I'd *killed* him. She was hysterical. All I could think about was getting Ruby away from there. So we just left. Charlie was waiting out in the car for me. He had no idea what was going on inside the house. Ruby was bawling her eyes out. I was just ... stunned ... and scared."

"Did you go to the police?" asked Annette. "Did you report it to someone?"

"Annette, I think I killed him ... the colonel. The thing is, Ruby told me he did this to a lot of other girls that they took in as foster children. And Mrs. Yates ... she was in on it. She didn't report any of his assaults on the girls. She's one of those mousy women who just look away and pretend it isn't happening. Colonel Yates was well respected. He was a decorated veteran and a pillar of the community. Who was going to believe *us?*"

Terry told Annette that they had gone to Charlie's house afterwards, where his friend had helped him gather up a few necessities in a backpack. Charlie's parents weren't home at that hour, so Terry decided to call his uncle in Wisconsin. He hoped his uncle would know what he should do.

"Uncle Will told me to bring Ruby to Madison. Charlie had a little money and gave me what he had. With the little bit in my wallet, I was able to buy bus tickets from Denver. Charlie couldn't take us to Denver, but he had a friend in college who was willing to drive us up. We left right away, before the police could come question Charlie's parents."

Annette got up to clear the table while Terry took a break from his long story. "So that's why the FBI is after you? Because you took Ruby and left the state?"

"I'm probably wanted for murder," said Terry. "I hate to think that I killed a man, Annette." He stood up and went to the look out the kitchen window. "If you'll let me stay in your barn tonight, I'll be gone in the morning."

"Where will you go?" asked Annette. "And a winter storm has moved in. Please, Terry … don't make any decisions right away. We'll think of something."

"I don't want to get you in trouble," he said. "Heck, I'm sure they've probably reached Uncle Will by now, and probably have Ruby in custody."

"Didn't you say he lives in Madison?" asked Annette.

"Yeah."

"Does your uncle drive a yellow station wagon?"

"Yeah." Terry looked at her curiously.

Annette looked him in the eye. "I think I saw them yesterday at the gas station right off the highway. Your uncle has blond hair and a mustache?"

He nodded.

"And I talked to your sister inside the gas station," she

added excitedly. She finished carrying the dishes from the table to the sink.

"You talked to Ruby?"

Annette quickly explained about why she was there and how Ruby had to wait for the restroom. "After seeing that photograph of her at the hut, I recognized her," she told him.

"Then they're in Ravensville," said Terry. "I wonder what that means."

"Does your uncle know anyone here?" asked Annette.

"Well, he works all around the state," said Terry.

"What does he do?"

"He's with the State Parks. He mostly works in the summer months."

"I see." Annette ran hot water in the sink and squirted in some detergent. When she heard Terry putting on his coat, she turned to him abruptly. "Terry, you're not staying in that barn. You can stay in the house with Mom and me. We have a spare bedroom upstairs."

"Oh, but your mom … what will she say?"

With a glance at the clock over the stove, Annette said, "She'll be home before midnight. After I do these dishes, we're going to go in the living room and watch a movie on TV. They've been running Christmas specials all week."

"Annette, are you sure?" Terry hung back, uncertain. "I mean, you could be harboring a fugitive."

"Nonsense," said Annette. "I'm not going to call the police, if that's what you mean. Let's wait till Mom gets home, and we'll see what she has to say about this."

"Okay," said Terry. "I'm looking forward to meeting Helen."

Annette looked over at him in surprise. "How did you know my mother's name?"

Terry didn't answer right away. He shook his head, smiled, then said, "I can read a telephone book."

Baffled by that response, Annette quickly washed the dishes, then left them to dry in the rack. She took Terry upstairs and showed him the bedroom he would sleep in, which was the spare room with the boxes piled against the walls. She eyed the box that the file folder had been in. She had been thinking about getting it out again and reading more about her father. No telling what else was in that file that she didn't know about him.

But while Terry set his pack down next to the closet, as she bent over to look for the file, she saw that it was no longer in the box. Her mother must have retrieved it. But why?

"Come on downstairs whenever you're ready," said Annette. She badly wanted to give Penny a call and say, "*Pen, guess what?*" But she realized that would be putting Terry Knutson in danger. He trusted her not to give him away, and until she learned more about his story—which she assumed was the truth—she had to be careful. She prayed her mother would get home early tonight. Surely Mom would know what to do.

The movie on television that night was Charles Dickens' *A Christmas Carol*. Annette had seen the film more than a few times, but always enjoyed it. A couple of times during the movie, she glanced over and noticed how tired Terry looked, sitting at the other end of the sofa and starting to nod off. When she suggested that maybe he should go up to bed, he just smiled and said that he preferred to wait till her mother got home.

During a commercial, Annette went and peeked out the curtains. The snow was still coming down. She hoped her mother wouldn't have any trouble driving home from the hospital.

When the movie ended at ten-thirty, Annette got up to turn the dial on the TV set to the other channel—they only got two—and sometimes a third channel that would come in fuzzy with a lot of static. The other channel had another late show in progress, so they watched that awhile.

Around eleven, Annette heard Ginger bark and she got up and went through the dining room into the kitchen. Mrs. Vetter came through the back door, shaking the snow off herself.

"Annette, I thought you'd be in bed by now. Boy, the roads are terrible. And it's so cold."

"Mom," said Annette, "there's somebody here."

Mrs. Vetter looked alarmed at first. "What? Who?"

Annette smiled. "It's okay. It's a friend."

Her mother removed her coat, and when she tried to hang hers up behind the door, she saw Terry's green parka hanging from one of the hooks and his boots on the linoleum. "Who is here?"

Annette beckoned to her mother, who followed her into the living room. Terry had stood up from the sofa and smiled at Mrs. Vetter. "Mrs. Vetter, I'm Terry Knutson."

"He needed a place to stay," explained Annette. "He was going to sleep in the barn ..."

"Terry ... *Knutson?*" Mrs. Vetter stared at him, not moving.

"He's been working for the Randts'," Annette continued. "I thought it was okay if he stays with us tonight. The storm and all ..." She was suddenly afraid that her mother would tell him to leave.

"Are you the one who's been trying to reach me at work?" asked Mrs. Vetter.

Annette looked from her mother to Terry, who nodded.

"Why would you call Mom at work?" she asked.

Mrs. Vetter sighed and went to turn off the television. She sat down in her rocking chair. "Sit down, you two. I want you to tell me what this is all about."

"Of course," said Terry. He sat back down, and Annette returned to her perch at the other end of the sofa. She listened carefully as Terry repeated his story to her mother. Nothing in the story changed. He told it exactly as he had revealed to her at the supper table.

When he was done, Annette asked again, "What did you want to call my mom for?"

Terry replied, "I came to Ravensville to try and find out if I had any relatives. My dad was from Ravensville."

"What?" Annette wrinkled up her nose. "He was?"

"Yeah," said Terry.

"Mom?" Annette looked for help from her mother.

"Knutson ..." Mrs. Vetter murmured, looking pale. "I don't know any people with that last name."

"Well, Knutson is my mother's maiden name," Terry explained. "I've been going by that name ever since I was born. You see, when my mother met Bob—my dad—I should say *step*dad—I used the name Foley for a while. Ruby's father is Bob ... Bob Foley, whom we believe was killed in Vietnam."

"Oh, dear," said Mrs. Vetter.

Ideas began to click inside Annette's brain. "That's why Ruby's name is Foley ... and yours isn't. Now I understand."

"Terry, I'm so sorry to hear about your family. But I don't see what this has to do with us."

"We don't know any Foleys either," added Annette.

"But you knew my uncle ... Will Knutson?" Terry looked inquisitively at Mrs. Vetter.

"Will Knutson ..." Then Mrs. Vetter remembered. "Oh. I believe he might have been a friend of my husband's."

"Hey, yeah, you did say your Uncle Will works for the State Parks," said Annette. "My dad was a ranger in Black River Falls."

"I know," said Terry.

"You do?" Annette's chin dropped.

"Will is my mom's brother," clarified Terry. "She was Ruth Knutson ... and then she became Ruth Foley when she married Bob, my stepdad. I always called him Dad because he was all I knew." Terry leaned back against the couch and folded his arms.

Annette noticed that her mother had suddenly grown very pale. Mrs. Vetter sank back into her rocker and stared into space.

"Mom, what's wrong?" cried Annette.

"Did you know my mom?" Terry asked.

"No ... no, I never knew her. I didn't want to know her." Mrs. Vetter cleared her throat. "You called me at work, wanting to know my husband's name and occupation and when he died ..."

"Yes," said Terry.

"Why?" she asked bluntly. "Please tell me the truth."

Annette thought her mother looked ready to cry. Somehow the name Ruth rang a bell in her brain.

"I may have gone by the name Knutson and Foley ... going back and forth over the years," said Terry calmly as he looked from one to the other of them. "But on my birth certificate, in Madison, Wisconsin, my name is recorded as Terence Thomas Vetter."

Both Annette and her mother let out loud gasps. Mrs. Vetter then let out a big sigh, but it was Annette who burst into tears and looked over at the boy sitting on the other end of the sofa. "Terry ... my dad was *your* dad. That makes you my half brother!"

15

Terry's Secret Revealed

By morning, a deep snow lay in rounded heaps outside the farmhouse as Annette climbed out of her bed and peeked outside the curtains. The wind was still blowing wispy drifts of white, although the flakes had stopped falling and the sky looked to be clearing.

She had hardly gotten any sleep. The three of them had stayed up and talked about Annette's father, Tom Vetter — who was now also Terry's father — and Mrs. Vetter had patiently answered Terry's questions about the kind of man Tom had been.

Finally exhausted, Terry had trudged upstairs to the spare room to get some sleep. Annette was wired, and emotionally drained like her mother. Although she went to her room shortly afterward, she couldn't get to sleep right away. She felt as though she were in some weird dream. Could it be true? Did she really have a brother? As wonderful as that could be, she couldn't accept the fact that her mother knew. How could she not have told Annette?

After she washed her face and got dressed, Annette went downstairs to the kitchen. She was surprised to find her mother at the table, drinking a cup of coffee. "Mom! What are you doing up?"

"I couldn't sleep," said Mrs. Vetter.

"Have you been up all night?" cried Annette.

"No, dear, I went up to bed. But I tossed and turned."

"Oh, me too," admitted Annette. She decided to try some coffee this morning and went to the cupboard to get a cup. Then she sat down beside her mother. "Mom, this whole thing blows my mind."

Mrs. Vetter sighed. "Oh, Annette … this was as much a shock to me as it is to you."

"You mean, you didn't know Dad had a son?"

"Of course not," said Mrs. Vetter.

"But you knew about his first wife … Ruth."

"Yes, he told me about her. I don't think your father even knew Ruth had his child."

"Mom, how is that possible?"

"Well," said Mrs. Vetter, "Ruth got an annulment just a couple of months after their marriage. She may not have known she was pregnant at the time. Whether she did or she didn't, for reasons known only to her, she did not inform your father."

"Yet his name was on the birth certificate," said Annette.

"Yes," agreed Mrs. Vetter. "She did declare Tom as the legal father. Let's see …" Mrs. Vetter did some mental calculations, then said, "Terry was born in March of the following year. Yes … his mother would have been two months along when the marriage ended."

"But then Terry said his mother married another man … Bob Foley … who was in the military."

"And that's the father Terry knew," said her mother. "He did say he only learned about his true paternity a short while ago. I guess he'd never laid eyes on his birth certificate until then."

"Gosh …" Annette stirred some sugar into her coffee cup.

"I have a brother ... I mean, a *half* brother ... it's what I've always wanted." She smiled, then sighed.

Mrs. Vetter reached a hand out and patted Annette's wrist. "For Terry's sake ... and most of all, for *your* sake ... I hope everything works out."

Annette recognized the trace of doubt on her mother's face and remembered the predicament Terry was in, regarding the assault in Colorado Springs. She sipped at her coffee, wishing she could call Penny and tell her the exciting news. But she couldn't tell Penny yet. She couldn't risk the authorities finding out that Terry was here at their house.

When Annette went out to milk Elizabeth, she saw right away that something was different in the barn. Alice was lying down in the straw, flinching every so often and then straining. Annette went over to check her.

Right away she could see that the cow's sides were sinking in and the heavy bulge with the calf had moved back toward the cow's tail end. The vulva was swollen and pink and Alice's udder was bulging with colostrum. Annette realized that it was happening at last—*Alice was in labor!*

Excited, Annette hurried to take care of Elizabeth's needs. When the milking was finished, she decided that the chickens could wait. She knew they weren't going to voluntarily leave the coop with all this snow, so Annette ran to the house to inform her mother about Alice.

"Really? She's going to have the calf today?"

"It sure looks that way, Mom. A little Christmas Eve calf!" Annette ran into the dining room.

"Where are you going?" called Mrs. Vetter.

"I've got to call Tim."

"Wait," cautioned Mrs. Vetter. "Do you have to call him *now?*"

"Oh." Annette stopped. She looked at her mother. "Terry."

"Right," said Mrs. Vetter.

"No one needs to know he's here," said Annette. "I'll call the Duncans after a while."

"It's going to take Alice a few hours anyway," said Mrs. Vetter.

"Yeah, you're right, Mom."

Ruby came down from the loft, where Uncle Will was stoking the fire. "Look outside, Uncle Will. It really snowed!" Ruby ran to the front window in the big living room.

"Don't act so surprised," said Uncle Will. "We get snow in Wisconsin too, you know."

"But it's *Christmas* snow," Ruby cried with delight. "And tonight is Christmas *Eve*."

"Yes, it is." He fed another stick of firewood onto the flames.

"Is Terry going to come to the cabin today?" asked Ruby.

Uncle Will sighed. "I honestly don't know how I'm going to drive the station wagon out of here, Ruby. There's a heck of a lot of snow to shovel first. The road is a long ways ..."

"But you've *gotta*," insisted Ruby. "It's going to be Christmas! And Terry doesn't even know we're here."

He could tell she was getting ready to shed tears, so he sighed, then stood up. "I'll do the best I can, girl. Come on and we'll fix some oatmeal this morning. I have instant packets. What flavor do you want—apples and cinnamon, or maple and brown sugar?"

Ruby hung her head and obediently followed her uncle over to the eating counter. She didn't have the heart to tell him she was pretty darn sick of that powdered milk. But it was kind of fun to toast a slice of bread on a stick over the flames in the fireplace. She knew Uncle Will had been strapped with a lot of responsibility since Terry had left her in his care. She didn't want to make life any harder for him.

The bell on the door jingled and Mr. Brown looked up from his work behind the counter. In walked the hippie couple, like they did every morning. "Almost like clockwork," he said out loud.

Maggie flashed the storekeeper a half-smile, then went immediately into the store's restroom while Stu started his usual walk down the aisles, looking at the different products on the shelves, stopping to study one thing and then another. Mr. Brown kept an eye on him.

"How's the snow out yer way? Did the plows make it through?"

Stu grunted in reply.

"You know, I can just about tell time by you two," Mr. Brown commented.

Stu jerked his head up and frowned. "What's that s'posed to mean?"

"The way you two come in every morning ... you're my best regulars."

The long-haired hippie sniffed and tried to ignore the older man.

"Take that lady of yours," continued Mr. Brown, his eyes shifting toward the restroom. "Why, she's quick to get to that washroom first thing. Don't you have running water out there where you live?"

This time he had irked the hippie man. Stu snorted. "Just what are you inferring, old man? That we live like pigs? Is that what you're saying?"

"Well, *you* said it ... not me."

Stu grabbed up some items of food and carried them over to the register. "I don't like your tone," he told Mr. Brown. "Maybe you should mind yer own business from now on."

"I'm just tryin' to be friendly," said Mr. Brown. He smiled, but it wasn't convincing.

Just then, Maggie barged out of the restroom. She pulled her coat tightly around her and came over to the counter with Stu. "Got any of those doughnuts this morning?"

"No doughnuts today," said Mr. Brown. "Sorry."

"Let's go, Maggie," said Stu, digging into his pocket for some money.

"Wait, Stu, I need some munchies." She started to turn around to search the potato chip aisle when something slipped to the floor with a plop. She quickly bent over and snatched it up, then stashed it into her coat pocket while Stu shot her a scornful look.

Mr. Brown had noticed, and they knew he had seen. But before he could say anything about it, the bell on the door jingled again, and in walked a large man in an overcoat, wearing a fur cap and sunglasses. "Good morning," Mr. Brown called to him.

The large man walked over to join them at the register and removed his sunglasses, wiping them on his coat sleeve. Then he immediately pulled out a badge, which he flashed before their three faces. "Name's Sam Chase. Federal Bureau of Investigation."

Right away Stu looked at Maggie and they slapped some bills down on the counter for Mr. Brown. "FBI, eh? Just a moment, sir. Let me get some change for these customers."

Stu grabbed up what he had purchased and the two of them flew out of the store. Both Mr. Brown and Sam Chase watched as the hippies jumped into their Jeep and drove away.

"Huh ... didn't even wait for his change," said Mr. Brown.

"I sometimes have that effect on some people," said the FBI agent.

"Well, what can I do for you, Mr. Chase?" Mr. Brown stuffed the money back into his cash drawer.

"I'm looking for a young man," said the agent. "Tall,

blond, unshaven ... name's Terry Foley. Sometimes he goes by the name Terry Knutson."

Mr. Brown looked startled. "You don't say ..."

"Do you know of him?"

"Why ... he was workin' here for me last week. Good worker, that kid." Then Mr. Brown leaned forward. "Tell me ... what did he do?"

"I'm afraid that's confidential." Sam Chase put away his badge and looked around. "Nice little country store you have here."

"There are good people here in this community," said Mr. Brown. "Hard-working, decent folks. Except those dang hippies!"

The FBI agent nodded in agreement, then whipped out a photo. "Seen this girl?"

Mr. Brown studied the picture carefully. She was a young teen-ager, blonde and pretty, wearing a red dress and red bows in her pigtails. "Can't say that I have," he confessed. "Nope. Haven't seen her."

"Can you tell me how I might find Terry Foley?" asked the agent.

"Of course. He went to work for Ron and Marge Randt at their dairy farm on Gaston Road."

"The Randt farm ... Brennan and I drove out there yesterday. The boy was gone."

"Oh." Mr. Brown nodded, puzzled by this news.

"Any idea where he might have gone after leaving that farm?"

Mr. Brown honestly had no idea. "Well, I do know one thing," he remembered.

"What's that?"

"He was stayin' out at the old water tower when he first got here. Maybe he went back there."

"Why the tower?"

"There's an old hut in the shadow of the tower," said Mr. Brown. "Used to be an old ranger's quarters, back in the day. A good place to hide out, I'd say." Then he added, "Terry's not a bad sort. Take my word for it. Whatever he's done ... you've got it wrong. You can bank on it."

Sam Chase put his sunglasses back on and headed for the door. "Thank you for the information, Mr. Brown." Then he left the store.

Mr. Brown drummed his fingers on the counter, suddenly worried. He had trusted that young man. What if he had been wrong? What if that young man had committed a terrible crime?

Inside the cabin, Ruby stewed and fretted. Uncle Will was outside, shoveling snow. She had done up the few amount of dishes as he had asked. She had brought in a couple of loads of firewood and it had been cold—a lot colder here in west-central Wisconsin than winter in Colorado Springs. She watched impatiently out the front window as her uncle kept shoveling, attempting to clear enough snow away to drive out onto the road with his station wagon. It didn't look like he was making a lot of progress.

"Maybe if I go out and help him," she told herself. She wrapped herself up in a blanket over her coat and stepped outside the cabin. There was only one shovel, unfortunately. But certainly there had to be something she could do to help.

"Go back inside," Uncle Will called to her. "You'll catch your death in this cold."

Ruby sighed, then plodded through the snow to where her snowman was half covered with new snow from last night's storm. The woods certainly looked beautiful from the snowfall. She wandered around to the back of the cabin, the sound of Uncle Will grunting and throwing heaps of snow aside filling the air.

As she came into view of a small clearing in back, she noticed something in the distance. It looked like the top of a tower of some kind. She shaded her eyes from the sun, which was now at treetop level at mid-morning. The tower was probably a mile away, from the looks of it. The sun hit it just right, so it reflected a bit off its bulbous top.

Suddenly, she heard Uncle Will yelling. She turned and ran around to the front of the cabin to see what was wrong. Uncle Will was leaning on the top of the snow shovel, one leg bent underneath him. He moaned in pain.

"Uncle Will! What's wrong?"

He looked up at her as she approached, his face contorted. "*Dang it* ... not again."

"What happened?" asked Ruby.

"It's that bum knee of mine," said Uncle Will. "I slipped, and I think I sprained my knee."

Ruby went over to him and put her arms around his waist. "Does it hurt bad?"

Uncle Will swore. He dropped the shovel to the ground. Then he tried to take a step, but when he put his weight on his left leg, he cried out and grabbed for Ruby's support, almost pulling her down.

"Oh, Uncle Will ... come on, I'll help you get to the house."

He grunted, then looked over at the car, which was covered up to the door handles in snow. "Well, okay, Ruby. But ... go slow ... *owwww.*"

She managed to help him get to the door of the cabin. He stumbled inside, rolling onto his back and clutching his left knee. Ruby was terrified at the look of pain on his face. "Uncle Will, we need to call for help," she said.

"There's no telephone, remember?" He gritted his teeth.

"Well, then ... I'll have to go for help," she said.

"No, Ruby, you can't do that." Panting, Uncle Will pulled

himself into a sitting position. "The road's too far away."

"Well, there were some other cabins before we got here," Ruby remembered. "Maybe someone is staying in them. I could go ask them for help."

Uncle Will was reluctant to let her go. He was worried about her freezing to death, for one thing, but also it would lead to questions ... and possibly authorities finding out who she was. "I'm sorry, darlin', I can't let you go," he said finally. "It's way too dangerous."

"What are we gonna do?" cried Ruby, growing more upset by the minute. "It's Christmas Eve, Uncle Will. You're hurt ... and what about Terry?"

She helped him get to the lawn chair with the blanket over it. With effort, he dragged himself into it and moaned. "Build the fire up, please," he directed. "Then bring another load of wood in for me. I'm probably going to regret this, but I'm going to let you try. You have to promise me you'll come right back here if there's nobody at that first cabin. I can't risk you getting stuck out there in this cold."

"I'll dress warmly, Uncle Will. I'll put on extra pants and I've got the boots you gave me, and my jacket and mittens."

She climbed up into the loft and brought the quilt down off of her bed. She wrapped it around her uncle, then went outside and brought in two extra loads of firewood. He was sitting close enough that he could—with effort, at least—keep it warm in the cabin until she returned.

"Get the pot on the stove," he directed. "Go outside and fill it with some snow. I'll put that on my knee for the swelling."

Ruby did as he told her, then bundled herself up as much as she could, making sure she would be protected from the wind and freezing temperatures. Then she hugged her uncle and planted a kiss on his forehead.

Tears filled her eyes. "I'm coming back, Uncle Will. Don't

worry. Everything will be fine."

He smiled, despite his pain and his fears. Then she hurried outside and pulled the door shut behind her. She knew she could find her way to the neighboring cabins. She just prayed that one of them was occupied.

W hen Terry came downstairs a little later that morning, Mrs. Vetter greeted him and asked if he wanted some breakfast. He smiled apologetically and hung his head. "Uh ... sure," he finally said. He looked around and asked, "Where's Annette?"

"She's out in the barn." Mrs. Vetter pulled a frying pan out of the lower cupboard. "One of her cows is giving birth today."

"Helen, I feel terrible about upsetting the two of you last night," said Terry.

"Oh ... don't worry about that now." She stood up and set the pan on the stove, then turned on the burner and faced him. "There's some coffee left. Sit down. I'll bring you a cup."

Terry sighed and took a seat at the kitchen table. "Thanks for letting me stay last night. I slept really great in that room."

Mrs. Vetter smiled at the young man. "We're happy to have you, Terry."

Terry stared down at his lap. "Makes it kinda hard to leave ... having found you and Annette ... and knowing who my dad was."

"Well, Annette is thrilled. She has wanted a brother or a sister for many years now," said Mrs. Vetter as she poured him a cup of coffee from the percolator. "Well, you'll see for yourself." She brought him the cup of coffee, then walked over to the refrigerator to get out some fresh eggs.

"I can't stick around," he mumbled. "Now that I have my answers ... I have to be on my way."

"Where will you go?" asked Mrs. Vetter. She looked at

him curiously.

"First, I have to see Ruby ... my half sister. I have to figure out what to do about her. It's unfair that Uncle Will got involved. He's always been a loner, you know."

Mrs. Vetter smiled. "Will Knutson was a good friend of Tom's. After our visit last night, I remembered more about him."

"Really?" Terry perked up. "I wonder why he didn't tell me. Uncle Will knew my dad when he was married to my mom? He's never told me that."

"Yes, I find that rather strange," commented Mrs. Vetter. "I'm sure he has his reasons."

"So you knew Uncle Will, too?"

"Not very well," admitted Annette's mother. "That seems like such a long time ago."

After he ate a breakfast of bacon, eggs and toast, Terry thanked Mrs. Vetter, then put on his parka and walked out to the barn, where he found Annette sitting in the straw beside her laboring cow. She jumped up as soon as he walked in.

"Hi, Annette." Terry smiled, his hands in his coat pockets.

"Terry, *hi!* See ... aren't you glad you didn't sleep in the barn? Alice is about to have her calf."

"Yes, I heard." He walked closer. The pregnant cow was having a contraction and he saw a yellow bag-like substance emerging from her behind. His eyes widened.

"That's the water bag," explained Annette. "It's the first thing to come out. Pretty soon, we'll see some front feet ... then the head."

"Wow ..." Terry's mouth fell open. He looked around and saw the other cow, munching on hay in her stall, her tail swishing. "How many cows do you have?"

"Two Holsteins," said Annette. "That's Elizabeth over there. Her sister, Alice, is having her second calf."

"Oh, then you're experienced at this." He smiled.

"Well, sort of. Not really." Annette explained how last year had been the first time Elizabeth and Alice had produced calves. "I got them for 4-H when they were heifers."

"What did you do with last year's calves?" asked Terry.

"Mr. Duncan down the road bought them from me." She grinned then and stood up. "This is going to be the best Christmas I've ever had in my life. My brother is going to be here with us."

Terry looked down at his feet.

"What's wrong?" asked Annette.

He sighed. "I can't stay, Annette."

"Oh, but why not?"

"I can't get you and Helen ... I mean, your mom ... in trouble because of me. I've got to leave."

"But ... but where will you go?"

"I haven't figured that out yet," said Terry.

The barn door swung open and Mrs. Vetter, dressed in her coat, called to Annette. "Penny's on the phone. Can you talk to her?"

Annette gasped. "Oh, gosh ... I don't know what to tell her." She turned to her mother. "Just tell her I'll call her later. I'm busy in here, Mom. Alice is having hard contractions."

"Do you want me to shovel your driveway for you?" Terry asked Mrs. Vetter.

"Why, that would be real good."

After Terry left the barn with her mother, Annette turned her attention back to Alice. She was concerned about what was going to happen to Terry now. If he left, she might never see him again.

Here she had just discovered her brother, only to have him run off. And then there was the question of his little sister, Ruby. What was to become of her?

16

Pumpkin Pie and a Note

Ruby's toes tingled from the cold and her cheeks were wind-burnt when she finally saw the neighboring cabin up ahead. The road was buried, but she had been able to follow it okay. It had just taken a long time, having to wade through two feet of snow. She noticed it wasn't as powdery and light as the Colorado snow she was used to. She prayed that someone was home at the cabin.

No car was in sight. The cabin had some smoke coming out of its chimney, though. That meant someone had been there. As she drew near, she could see that a vehicle had been parked there earlier. Its tracks led out the half-plowed driveway toward the highway, which was still a ways away.

Ruby went to the door and knocked. "Anybody home?" she called, and knocked several more times.

Not willing to give up, she waded through a drift of snow to peer into a window, but it was too dark inside to see anything. Finally, she went back to the door and tried it. To her surprise, the cabin was not locked and she walked right in.

This cabin was just as rustic as the one she and Uncle Will were staying in, but at least it had more furnishings. There was also a Christmas tree, all decorated, in the corner, and some gifts that were wrapped under the tree. There was a beautiful oak dining table, upon which there were pies that were cooling and a loaf of fruitcake somebody had baked.

Ruby noticed a nice couch, a bear rug and some bookshelves. She suddenly envied the people who stayed here. A sob escaped her throat.

She didn't know what to do, whether she should wait here for somebody to return, or if she should go on to the next place … and get help for Uncle Will. After all, he was in tremendous pain.

Because she was cold and hungry, Ruby warmed herself next to the fire, which still had a large log smoldering, and even added a couple of smaller logs. Then she looked over at the table and just couldn't help herself. It was probably her only chance of having some Christmas pie.

Poking around in the kitchen area, she found a plate in the cupboard and a fork and knife. She cut herself a slice of the pumpkin pie, then sat down in front of the fire and enjoyed it.

Half an hour passed and nobody had returned to the cabin. Ruby decided she couldn't wait any longer. She noticed a stack of Christmas card envelopes on the counter and a pencil on the bookshelf. She scribbled a note on the back side of an envelope:

Thank you for the pie. Merry Christmas!

Then she tucked the envelope under the pie tin, bundled herself up again, and left the cabin.

Outside in the wind, Ruby covered her mouth with the scarf and looked up at the tree line. There she could see the old water tower again. This time it seemed closer. She knew that if she somehow got lost, she would probably be able to find her way back to Uncle Will because she had the tower in sight.

With the spicy, sugary taste of pumpkin pie in her mouth, Ruby started out in the direction of the highway, hoping that the next cabin or house she got to would be occupied.

A lice was straining with her labor in the barn. Mrs. Vetter had come out to see how Annette was doing. Terry was still shoveling the driveway so that she could get out and drive to work.

"Mom, we can't let Terry leave yet," said Annette. "Please, can't he stay here?"

Mrs. Vetter was obviously distressed by the situation with Terry. She looked so tired and worn out. "We can't really stop him," she said.

"But where will he go? Tomorrow's Christmas."

"Annette, the authorities are looking for him."

"But he didn't do anything wrong," insisted Annette.

"Do we really know that?" Mrs. Vetter looked at her daughter. "Do you really trust him?"

Annette couldn't believe what she was hearing. "Mom!"

Alice mooed loudly, and Annette got back to work with the cow.

"Look, I think I see a foot," said Mrs. Vetter. "Isn't that one of the hooves?"

"Yes." Annette grinned. "Yes, it is!" She knew the calf would be born soon.

"Well, I'd better go back to the house and get ready for work," said Mrs. Vetter. "Terry asked me to drive him into town."

"Mom ... please ... don't let him go," begged Annette.

Mrs. Vetter only sighed, then headed for the barn door.

Annette watched as the cow had another contraction. The hoof pushed its way out just a little, and then retracted. She knew this might go on for some time, but she didn't want to miss the event.

She also did not want to see her new brother — now that she knew him — depart from her life. But she knew Terry had to do what he thought was best. Still, it was all so unfair.

There was another house up ahead, back a ways from the woods. Ruby's teeth chattered, she was so cold. She saw that this house was not a cabin, but a green farmhouse that looked pretty shabby from the outside. An old blue Jeep, also not in good shape, was parked at the road. Whoever lived in the farmhouse had not bothered to clear the driveway. It looked like she might have come to the county highway. Excited at the progress she was making to help Uncle Will, Ruby plowed her way through the snow as quickly as possible and pounded on the front door.

It was a whole minute before someone opened the front door just a crack. Right away, Ruby's nostrils were assaulted by a pungent, smoky odor that filled the house. The man who stood at the door, looking down at her, was tall and greasy-looking, with stringy black hair, a beard and piercing dark eyes.

"Who's at the door, Stu?" a woman's voice called from within.

"I dunno," he replied, a wicked kind of smile folding the skin on his pale face. She noticed he had dark circles under his eyes. "Must be one of Santa's elves."

"Please," cried Ruby, "my uncle's in trouble. I need to call for help."

A heavyset, smaller woman came into sight next. She wore a long-sleeved shabby dress that reached down to her bare feet. A beige-colored shawl hung around her shoulders and her hair was long, red and frizzy. She stared at Ruby in astonishment, her cheeks ruddy and pudgy looking. "My goodness," she said and placed her hands on her hips. "What have we here?"

Stu pulled Ruby into the room and closed the door. Maggie looked out the window, as if she expected to find someone else out there.

Ruby was glad to be inside, where it was warm, but she wasn't sure about these people. The smoke-filled room was overwhelming. She noticed a couple of incense sticks burning, and there was a wood stove in the corner. The place was a mess, with paper trash, clothing and food packages thrown in every corner. A couple of tabby cats were stretched out in front of the stove, soaking up the heat.

"Do you … do you have a telephone I can use?" asked Ruby, looking around for one.

"Who are you going to call, girl?" asked Stu.

"I … I don't know," she confessed.

"Who's your uncle?" demanded Maggie.

"Uncle Will," said Ruby.

"Where did you come from?" she asked next.

"Our cabin … about a mile or so from here … in the woods."

Stu and Maggie looked at each other, and then Maggie ushered Ruby over to a flimsy couch. She brushed a pile of newspaper pages off onto the dirty floor and told her, "Sit." Then she grabbed Stu and led him off into another room, which Ruby guessed was their kitchen. Strings of colored beads hung over the doorway. She could hear them talking, but they purposely kept their voices low.

Finally, Stu came out and stood with his head cocked, studying her. "We don't have no phone," he said. "We can't call anyone."

"Well then …" Ruby rubbed the end of her nose. "Can you … can you take me somewhere? I need to find someone who can help my uncle."

"Why? What's wrong with your uncle?" asked Maggie.

"He … he hurt himself shoveling snow. He sprained his knee."

"Do you live around here?" asked Maggie.

"Why… no," said Ruby. "We're just … just visiting … staying in the cabin for … for Christmas." She did not want to have to explain the truth of her situation. Besides, these people were hippies and she was quite sure they were smoking marijuana, which was why the house smelled funny.

Maggie confronted Ruby in a threatening manner, her arms once again on her fat hips. "We don't believe you, girl."

"Who sent you here?" demanded Stu, a mean look in his piercing eyes.

"But I … oh, please, mister … nobody sent me here."

"And where is this uncle of yours?" asked Maggie.

"I told you … back at the cabin. It's the last one, way out on the far side of the woods."

"Well, whose cabin is it?" asked Stu.

Ruby didn't remember Uncle Will's friend's name. She just shrugged her shoulders and shrank back from the man as he bent forward in a threatening manner.

"What's your name?"

Ruby hesitated. Her eyes darted around the room, seeking a means of escape. She had a feeling this wasn't going to end well for her. Visions of her recent skirmish with Colonel Yates and his stand-by, do-nothing wife—her supposed foster parents—filled her with panic, all of a sudden.

She needed to get away. Her instincts told her these people could not be trusted. She didn't know what this man might try to do to her. She had trusted Colonel Yates … and he had molested her.

"You're scaring her, Stu." Maggie sighed and pushed the man back. She sat down on the couch next to Ruby and started to remove her scarf and her coat. "Never mind him. He's paranoid. Here, take off those things … get warm. Then we'll decide what to do about you."

Ruby flinched at the woman's touch and shifted herself to the far end of the couch.

"She's skittish." Stu laughed.

"I'm not gonna hurt you," insisted Maggie, more annoyed than she was kind.

"I'll go," said Ruby, starting to get up from the couch. "I've got to find someone who can help Uncle Will."

"No, *stay here.*" Maggie's voice hardened. "Goodness, you're half frozen. I'll go make you some tea. Stu, you make sure she sits there. Don't let her leave this house." Maggie, in her bare feet, stumbled her way into the kitchen.

Now Ruby was more scared, but she didn't dare let on. She sat back down and stayed quiet.

Stu kept staring at her, that leer on his face that frightened her more than Maggie's harsh tone. "After some of Maggie's tea, you'll be feelin' just fine," he promised. "Just fine, little girl."

"What ... what kind of tea is she making?" asked Ruby suspiciously. She didn't like the lusty look in his beady eyes.

"Oh, Maggie's brew always works wonders," promised Stu. "Whoever sent you here, they're gonna be disappointed. We're not gonna let you rat us out."

Suddenly, Ruby realized she had to get out of this farmhouse. There was no telling what these hippies were going to drug her with. But she had to play it cool, or the same thing would happen to her that it did in Colorado Springs. This time she had to play it smart. *She had to save herself.*

Annette was getting nowhere with Alice. The calf's hoof kept poking out, then getting sucked back in. Half an hour had passed since her mother had been out in the barn. She went to the barn door and looked out. Terry was just finishing the driveway, the part down by the road, next to the mailbox. She knew her mother was getting ready and would leave — and with Terry — within minutes.

"Hang on, Alice," Annette called to her cow, who was

obviously in discomfort with her fidgeting and straining movements. Annette made her way to the house and, without taking off her boots or her coat, made her way to the telephone in the dining room.

No one answered when she dialed the Duncans' number. That didn't seem right. Where were they? She thought about giving Pete a call, but then realized there wasn't time ... and how was Pete going to get over to her house when he didn't drive, and most likely the roads were still not cleared?

Just then, Terry came in through the kitchen door, looking sweaty and tired. Annette hung up the receiver and stared at him, worried.

"What's wrong, Annette?" he asked.

"Everything," she confessed. "Alice is having a difficult birth, and I can't reach Penny or Tim."

"Is there anything I can do to help?"

"Probably not," said Annette, then suddenly changed her mind. Maybe she could delay Terry enough so that when her mother had to leave for the hospital, he wouldn't go with her. She desperately needed Terry to stay with them a little longer. "Yes, actually, I *could* use your help," she told him. "Come on, let's go out to the barn, and I'll show you."

Together they took off for the barn, Terry anxious to be of help with the calving, but Annette worried sick that the calf would have to be turned first.

"I've got to admit, Pen, this was one of your better ideas." Tim sat behind the steering wheel of his blue Chevelle as he and his sister backed down the plowed driveway of the Randt farm. "I'm sure Pete and his family really appreciate getting those goodies you baked."

Penny smiled, enjoying the feeling of satisfaction she had after delivering the box of treats to all those cute Randt children. "But the best part was Mom and Dad letting them have that side of beef. I think Mrs. Randt was in tears when we told her we're giving them all that meat."

"That's what Christmas is all about," agreed Tim. "Neighbors helping neighbors."

"And heaven knows, the Randt family can use it," said Penny.

"Your peanut butter fudge turned out okay this year," said Tim.

"Yeah." Penny laughed. "Better than last year's batch. Remember?"

"You mean that disgusting concoction that looked like something in the calf barn? That was the pits."

"Oh, you don't have to be so *gross*." A moment later, she said, "Maybe we should stop at Annette's on the way home. She never called me back, you know."

"Hmm," said Tim. He turned onto Gaston Road and was heading north toward home. "That is kind of strange."

"Her mom sounded kind of funny on the phone," Penny added.

"What do you mean?" asked Tim.

"Well, you know ... stressed out."

"Is that unusual?"

"I dunno. Annette's been kind of worried about her mom the last few weeks. She thinks her mom's depressed."

"Like in ... holiday blues?"

"Something more than that, I'm afraid," said Penny.

"We'll drop by," Tim assured her.

As they turned onto Tower Drive, Penny called out, "Tim! Stop!"

He had already seen it. He swerved and then skidded, just missing a young person bundled up in winter wear and men's pants. The Chevelle slid to a stop on the side of the slippery road.

Penny's hand clutched her heart and her green eyes grew

wide with disbelief. "Well, thank goodness you swerved in time. You almost hit that person."

Tim wasted no time. Leaving the motor running, he opened the door and climbed out of the car. "Hey!" he called out. A girl turned to look at him, but didn't move. Tim ran over to her and saw that her face was stained with tears and a scratch on her chin had drawn some blood. She had been crying.

Penny jumped out of the car and ran over. "We didn't hit you, did we?" she asked the girl.

The girl stared, unable to speak. She was out of breath, as if she had been running. "Can you ... can you ... please ... help me?" She broke out into sobs.

"Tim, let's get her into the car," said Penny. Together, they helped the teen-ager over to the Chevelle and let her into the back seat. Then they climbed in and turned around to look at her.

"Oh, my gosh," cried Penny as she recognized their passenger. "You're ... you're Ruby."

The girl looked even more frightened. She wanted to get out, but she couldn't, since the Chevelle was a two-door and they were both sitting in the front seat, blocking her way.

"Ruby who?" Tim was puzzled and stared at his sister.

"It's Terry's sister," Penny told him. She smiled at the girl. "It's all right. We know Terry."

At once, the girl relaxed and buried her head in her hands, sobbing with relief. "Yes ..." she cried. "Yes, I'm Ruby Foley. Please ... Can you take me to him? Do you know where he is? My uncle sprained his knee at the cabin ... and he needs help."

"Where is your uncle?" asked Penny.

Ruby just cried.

"What happened to you?" asked Tim. "Where did you get that scratch on your face?"

Overwhelmed, Ruby couldn't speak for a full minute. But then she told them what had happened. It had been another traumatic situation, but this time she had gotten away.

When Stu and Maggie were sitting in the corner of their living room, discussing how they were going to deal with her intrusion on them, Ruby had put on her coat and scarf, and then had gone and picked up one of their cats lying beside the fire. She had stroked the big tom and held him in her lap on the couch while the adults were conferring.

Then, when Maggie heard the tea kettle in the kitchen and went to make the tea for Ruby — apparently a drugged brew — Ruby had taken her chance.

Carrying the big tom in her arms, she raced for the front door. When Stu had cried out and tried to block her from leaving, she had tried to toss the cat at him, as a distraction to get away. But the frightened animal had clung to Ruby instead and scratched her chin before she was able to get the animal off of her. As soon as she could, she had run out the door.

"I ran as fast as I could through that snow," she told Tim and Penny. "I *had* to get away. And I did." She explained that once she was up on the highway, she just kept running. She figured she would meet a passing car eventually — and, thankfully, she had.

"What house was it where you escaped from?" asked Penny.

"It was a green farmhouse," said Ruby. "It was down a side road."

Tim nodded his head and gave his sister a look. "I'll bet that's the one Annette and I went to a few days ago."

"And the couple ... they must have been Stu and Maggie," guessed Penny.

"Yes, that was their names. They were doing drugs," said Ruby. "They thought someone had sent me to catch them ... and that I was going to rat on them. I was so scared!" More tears spilled from her eyes.

"Let's get her home," said Penny.

"Do you ... know where ... Terry is?" Ruby managed to utter between sobs.

Penny put a comforting hand on Ruby's arm as Tim swung the car back onto the road and continued driving toward Tower Drive. "I'm afraid not, Ruby. You see, he was working at the farm of one of our friends ... but he left there yesterday morning ... and no one's seen him since."

"We need to get help for Uncle Will," insisted Ruby, struggling to stay collected. After all, these two people were on her side. They were obviously not going to turn her in or report her to the police. Besides, they knew Terry. They just didn't know where he was.

"Let's get to the nearest telephone," said Tim.

"That would be the Vetters'," said Penny. She smiled at the girl. "It's going to be all right. You're safe with us."

Ruby sank back against the back seat of Tim's car. For the first time in days, she felt some relief. Yet it wasn't over. Uncle Will still needed help, and most of all ... she needed to find Terry.

17

A Calf is Born

When Tim pulled into the Vetters' driveway several minutes later, Mrs. Vetter was just heading for her car. She wore her winter coat, boots, and carried her bag of knitting. The car was warmed up in the newly cleared driveway, with exhaust coming out from behind. She stopped when she saw them.

"Mrs. Vetter, you've got to help us," said Penny, who was the first to step out of the Chevelle.

"I was just leaving for the hospital," she said. "Is everything okay?"

Tim opened his door and said, "We need to use your telephone."

"Good heavens, what's wrong?" Mrs. Vetter stepped forward, then halted when she saw the blond girl riding in the back seat. "Who is that with you?"

"That's a girl we picked up on the road," said Penny.

"Her uncle is hurt," explained Tim. "We have to get him some help."

"Someone is injured?" Mrs. Vetter's face grew serious. She peered into the window of the car and gasped when she saw Ruby's scratched-up face. "Let's get her inside right away.

What happened? Were you in an accident?"

"No," said Penny, and explained how they had found Ruby running along Gaston Road, and how Tim had swerved on the icy pavement.

"Oh no, you didn't hit her?" cried Mrs. Vetter in alarm.

Tim pulled his seat forward and reached his hand out to Ruby, who slowly crawled out onto the driveway. Tears welled up in her eyes. "No, a cat scratched her," he said. "Ruby, this is Mrs. Vetter. She's a nurse."

Mrs. Vetter had heard the name and was instantly alert, but she showed no reaction. "Come on, dear. Don't worry, I'm going to take care of you. It's all right."

"Where is Annette?" asked Penny, looking around.

Mrs. Vetter stiffened suddenly and didn't answer.

"I'll bet she's in the barn," said Tim.

"No! Wait!" Then Mrs. Vetter smiled apologetically. "Help me get this girl into the house first."

Penny and Tim looked at each other uncertainly. It wasn't like Annette's mom to act this strangely, but they followed her inside the Vetters' kitchen, where Ruby took a seat at the kitchen table. Penny helped the girl remove her coat and the pair of man's pants she was wearing to keep warm.

Mrs. Vetter soon came out of the downstairs bathroom with some first aid items. Soon she was crooning over Ruby and getting more of the story as the girl explained that she had walked two or three miles, through the heavy snow, to find help for her uncle, who had sprained his knee at the cabin in the woods. She then repeated the story of how the two hippies, Stu and Maggie, had tried to keep her from leaving their farmhouse, for fear she was going to tell the police about their drug use.

"We need to get to that man … her uncle," Mrs. Vetter said to Tim. "Can you drive me there?"

"Well, my car won't be able to get through the snow,"

explained Tim. "I'll have to run home first and get the truck."

"Ruby will have to go along," said Penny. "She knows the way."

Ruby nodded eagerly. "The cabin's on the other side of that old tower. I could see it through the tops of the trees."

"I think I know where those cabins are," said Tim.

Suddenly, the back door swung open and a man's voice called, "Helen? Helen, Annette needs to call Tim. There's a problem with the ..." He stopped as soon as he saw the people gathered in the kitchen, and then his eyes rested on his sister Ruby, seated at the table.

"Terry!" Ruby burst into tears at the sight of her brother. Mrs. Vetter had to jerk away as the girl sprang to her feet and ran to the boy who had come through the door.

"Ruby ... what are you doing here?" Terry caught her in his arms and hugged her tightly. "Oh, Ruby ... what happened to you?" He pulled away and stared at her face.

Tim went to the door and turned to face Terry. "Annette's in the barn?"

"Yes," said Terry. "She wanted me to call you. The calf is turned wrong."

Tim flew out the door and Penny was at his heels as they raced to the barn. When they came barging in, Annette cried out, "Oh, thank God! Tim! Penny! The calf!" She had tears streaming down her cheeks. She knelt beside Alice, who was mooing and flailing on her side in the straw.

Reddish gunk was oozing out of the cow's rear end. The water bag, which was draped over the hooves that dangled out of the opening, had broken already. Tim asked Annette for some disinfectant. She had her medicines and instruments on a chair next to the stall. Then she handed Tim the shoulder-length rubber gloves that she had saved with her other equipment. He washed, then pulled on the gloves and bent down to help the suffering cow.

Penny, who was squeamish about such things, hung back and rubbed Annette's shoulders as they watched Tim go to work, carefully easing his hand in between the cow's birth canal and the unborn calf.

"I'm so glad you showed up," said Annette. She glanced toward the barn door, expecting Terry to follow. When he didn't, she said, "You know he's here?"

"Terry?" asked Penny, and nodded. "Why didn't you tell me?"

"I couldn't," said Annette.

"How long has he been here?" asked Penny.

"He showed up last night."

"Last night!" Penny looked stricken. "Annette!"

"I didn't want to take a chance ..." said Annette. "The FBI and all ..."

"Ruby's inside," Penny told her.

"What!" Now it was Annette's turn to be surprised. "What's Ruby doing here?"

While Penny quickly explained the circumstances, they watched as Tim very skillfully was able to turn the calf to the correct position for it to move the rest of the way down the birth canal. She was still explaining about the implications with Stu and Maggie at the green farmhouse when suddenly the calf's head poked out. After another couple of pushes on Alice's part, the calf dropped all the way out onto the straw, along with a small gush of blood and mucus.

"The calf is out!" shouted Annette.

They watched Tim clean the mucus from the calf's nose and mouth, using a bulb syringe. Then he reached down and retrieved a piece of straw off the floor and tickled the inside of its nose.

A tiny sneeze came from the calf. Tim picked it up and gently held the baby animal by its hind legs and swung it briefly upside down. This cleared more mucus from its throat.

When he placed the calf back on its feet, it wobbled a little, but was able to stand on its own. Big brown eyes took in the calf's first look at its world.

"Oh, Tim, thank you! Thank you!" Annette rushed over to the tall, dark-haired boy and threw her arms around him. "You saved the day."

Tim held her a moment, then smiled as he removed the messy gloves and dropped them onto the barn floor. They watched as the new little calf, with its dangling umbilical cord, staggered some more and then tried taking a couple of wobbly steps. "Looks like you've got a little bullock."

"It's a boy," confirmed Penny.

"He's so cute," said Annette.

Alice pulled her heavy, weary cow body up off the straw and stood, then looked around to gaze at her baby.

"I wish you'd called me over sooner," said Tim.

"I tried," insisted Annette. "Nobody was home."

"Mom and Dad took Karen to see Santa Claus in town," explained Penny.

They watched as Alice began licking and cleaning the little calf with her big tongue.

"And where were *you?*" asked Annette.

"Tim drove me out to take some candy and cookies to the Randts'," added Penny.

"That's when we came across Ruby on the road," said Tim.

"Your mom's inside, and they're getting ready to go get Ruby's uncle at the cabin," said Penny.

"Uncle?" asked Annette.

Penny quickly explained what she knew.

The little calf had made his way over to Alice and was seeking her teats for his first meal of some nourishing colostrum. The antibodies in the substance were critical for the calf's well being, they knew.

"They'll be fine now," said Tim. "Let's go to the house."

The three of them hurried out of the barn and, when they got inside the Vetters' house, Ruby was beaming with happiness now that she had found her brother, and Terry turned to face Annette, Tim and Penny. "Helen said she'd drive us over to your farm," he told Tim.

"Okay. I hope Dad's back from town with the truck by now."

Mrs. Vetter, who had gone into the bathroom to clean up, came out. "Oh, my! I'd better call the hospital and tell them I'm going to be late."

"No time for that," said Tim. "Come on." Then he said, "Annette, can you call the hospital?"

"I'm staying here?" she asked.

"There's not enough room in the truck for everybody," said Tim. "You and Penny had better stay. There's room for your mom, Ruby and Terry ... and then we'll have to cram her uncle in somehow."

Annette and Penny agreed to stay at the house, although it was killing Annette not to be in on the adventure. After everyone left, she promptly called the hospital to report her mother would be late. Then, she and Penny stood in the kitchen, unable to speak at first.

Then, Annette broke the silence. "Oh, Pen, I feel rotten about not calling you."

Penny crossed her arms. "You should! Don't you trust me — your own best friend? Did you think I was gonna call that FBI guy ... or Detective Brennan? Annette, you know me better than that."

"I do," said Annette. "Honest, I do, Pen. It's just ... I didn't want to get you guys involved, just in case Terry was a criminal."

"But he's not ... *is he?*" Penny's eyebrow lifted as she stared at Annette.

Annette then filled her friend in on what Terry had told

them last night, about how he had found the foster dad in Colorado Springs trying to hurt his sister, and how they had fought and Terry had ended up knocking the older man to the floor and was afraid he'd killed him.

"Well, is he dead?" asked Penny.

"He didn't wait around to find out," said Annette.

"*Well* ..."

"But since the FBI is after him ... Then again, maybe it's because he crossed state lines with a minor ... his sister Ruby. Not because he killed someone ... though, I must admit, we don't know for sure yet." Annette trembled and sat down on one of the kitchen chairs. She suddenly felt extremely fatigued and buried her face in her arms. "If anything happens to him ... oh, God, please ... don't take Terry away from me."

Penny pulled out the chair next to Annette and stroked her arm. "Annette ... you really care for him, don't you?" Her voice was soft. As her friend cried softly into her arms, Penny started piecing things together in her head. "Poor Pete ... poor, poor Pete ..."

Annette's head jerked up and she stared with swollen, red eyes. "What? Oh, *you* think ... No! You've got it wrong, Penny."

"It's okay, Annette. I understand now."

"But, Pen ... you see ..."

Suddenly, Ginger jumped up and started barking.

"Someone's here." Penny jerked up from the table and looked out the kitchen window. "Oh, no ... it's Detective Brennan!"

Annette jumped to her feet. She could see that her mom's car was gone. *Thank goodness.*

"Detective Brennan ..." Annette opened the door to let him in.

"Hello, Annette." Bob Brennan entered the kitchen and bent over to give Ginger a pat on his red head. The collie swished his tail slowly and sniffed the detective's boots. "Hello, Penelope. How are you doing?"

Penny cringed at the formal expression of her name. "I'm fine. Merry Christmas."

"Merry Christmas to you, too." Bob Brennan smiled. "Is your mom home?"

"No, she went ..." Annette stopped herself.

"Oh, that's right, she works nights at Ravensville General. I forgot. Well, at least you have Penny here to keep you company on Christmas Eve."

"Uh ... what brings you out here, Detective?" Annette was aware that her eyes were still wet, but she displayed a convincing smile.

"The FBI sent an agent up here to try to find a missing little girl and her brother. We got wind that he was working out at the Randt farm. His name's Terry Foley ... sometimes goes by Terry Knutson. Have you seen him?"

Annette composed herself and licked her lips. "Yes, I met him ... out at the Randts' last week. I had to take Pete's home-work to him. He got bronchitis and had to stay out of school."

"I see." Bob Brennan rubbed his chin, then looked from Annette to Penny, then asked, "Well, we're also on the lookout for a blond little girl, about 13, who was seen riding around in a yellow station wagon with a man we presume to be her uncle from Madison. His name's Will Knutson. The girl's name is Ruby Foley."

Both Annette and Penny stared at the detective without any expression on their faces. Then they looked at each other and shrugged. Nothing more.

"What does the FBI want with him, anyway?" Penny finally asked the detective.

"Actually, Sam Chase left this afternoon," the detective revealed. "It seems Terry Knutson left town yesterday. The Randts don't think he's coming back. As a matter of fact, Sam drove down to Madison. His family's there, so he's spending Christmas with them. Then he'll see if the uncle shows up with his niece."

"But what did Terry *do?*" Annette tried to act innocent and flashed her eyelashes at him.

"Oh ... there's an assault charge. I guess it wouldn't do any harm to tell you, now that we think he's left the area. He had an altercation with a retired Air Force colonel. The guy and his wife were foster parents to Ruby, his sister. There was some kind of fight, I understand. Terry fled the scene."

"Well ... what happened to the ... victim?" Penny swallowed.

Detective Brennan shook his head and stuck out his lower lip. "He's in the hospital."

"He didn't die?" asked Annette.

"Not that I know of," said Bob Brennan. "Well, girls, I'd best be getting along. I just thought I'd check, since he might have come around looking for a job." He turned around to go out the door, then stopped and looked at Annette. "Be sure to let me know if you should see any of them." Then he smiled.

"Just a minute." Annette stepped forward and the detective halted.

Penny pulled on Annette's arm, but she ignored her friend.

"Have you checked out that green farmhouse off Gaston Road?" Annette asked. "You remember ... I called you last week about it ..."

"Why? Do you think there's a connection?" asked Bob Brennan.

Penny was shaking her head "no" at Annette, which tipped off the detective.

Detective Brennan asked, "You'd better tell me what you know, Annette. I see that look."

Suddenly, Annette broke down. "I'm sorry ... I'm so

sorry, Detective Brennan."

"Call me Bob."

"You need to go check out that house," she said between sobs.

"Why?"

"Because ... that little girl was there ... this afternoon."

Penny threw her arms up in frustration and turned around in a circle. "You might as well tell him the whole story, Annette."

And so Annette ended up telling Bob Brennan *part* of the story—not the entire thing. She told him about how Tim and Penny had found Ruby running alongside the road that afternoon. Then she explained how they had brought Ruby to the house and Mrs. Vetter had nursed the cat scratch that she had received when she tried to escape.

But Annette purposely left out the part about Terry showing up and being reunited with his sister. She was glad Penny did not fill in that part.

Detective Brennan did not chastise them for not telling him right away. Instead, he told them to get their coats on. He wanted them to come with him.

"Is he arresting us?" Penny looked so worried, Annette thought her friend was going to cry.

"I don't know, Pen." Annette got into her coat again, and when they were ready, they walked outside to the detective's sedan. He was radioing in a call to the Sheriff's Department.

Reluctantly, the girls climbed into the back seat of Bob's car, and then they were on the road, headed back toward Tower Drive and Gaston Road, and the lane where they had once been taken last October, in the back of Dave Beck's camper—and where Annette, with Pete's cousin Luke, had discovered a drug bash happening the night of the Homecoming game.

Annette noticed there were no vehicles at the farmhouse,

but they could see that one had been there recently because there were tire tracks in the snow. They waited on the road outside the driveway of the green farmhouse for several minutes, until a sheriff's patrol car pulled up beside them. Two deputies got out. Detective Brennan and the girls waited in his car while the two officers went to the door. They knocked, but there was no response.

"No one appears to be home," said one of the officers when they returned to the road. "We don't have a warrant. We can't break in without one."

"Oh, great," grumbled Annette, "looks like they've gotten away again."

"Who were these two people?" Bob had pulled out his notebook to write down some information.

"All we know is their first names ... Maggie and Stu."

"You might talk to Mr. Brown," said Penny. "They come into his store a lot. They were there that one time that you and I were there, Annette."

"That's right," said Annette.

"I'll do that," said Bob. "I'd better take you two home."

"False alarm," one of the deputies said as the two men went to their squad car and took off.

"Are we in trouble?" asked Annette, when Bob pulled into the Vetters' driveway.

The detective turned to face them with a smile. "I don't think this warrants an arrest. But instead, I want you to promise me ... you'll call me as soon as your mother returns with Ruby Foley and her uncle. I'm heading over to the hospital now, in case they took him there."

Annette gulped. "Fair enough."

After he dropped them off, Penny waited in the house while Annette ran out to the barn to check on Alice and her new calf. The two were doing well, so she decided it was time to go ahead and get Elizabeth milked and the chickens taken care of, while she could.

By the time she went back to the house, Tim had just pulled into the driveway and Penny was already outside to greet the returning party.

"Oh, they're back," Annette said to herself as she walked from the barn to the truck. She could see Uncle Will sitting up front with Tim and Terry. Her mother drove up beside the truck, with Ruby beside her in the Vetters' car, which they had taken and left at Duncans' when they got the truck.

Annette sighed and told herself, "I promised Bob I'd call. But if I do, Terry is doomed."

18

Christmas Eve

The sun was down behind the trees. Annette waited beside Ruby, Penny and her mother while Tim and Terry helped Uncle Will out of the truck. Supported by their shoulders, he limped along as the three of them headed for the farmhouse. Annette and the others followed them as they took Uncle Will into the living room and settled him onto the couch, where he would be more comfortable.

Ginger greeted everyone eagerly. Once they got Uncle Will situated, Penny plugged in the Christmas tree lights and Ruby gasped at the beauty of the tree. Annette could see that the girl's blue eyes danced at the sight. She had a lovely smile.

"There's no sense in my going to work now," said Mrs. Vetter a few minutes later as she filled the tea kettle with fresh water from the tap and set it on the electric stove to heat up. "I'm going to call the hospital."

"Oh good, Mom," said Annette, "you're going to be home for Christmas Eve after all."

"I'll only go in if they really need me." She patted Annette's arm. "Will has a bad sprain, but we can treat it here just fine."

Annette understood her mother's meaning. They weren't

going to alert the authorities as to the man's whereabouts—nor Ruby's, for that matter.

"Mom, I've got to tell you," said Annette. "Detective Brennan was here earlier."

Annette filled her mother in on how Detective Brennan had driven Penny and herself over to the farmhouse off Gaston Road, where the hippies lived. She explained how the sheriff's deputies arrived, but no one appeared to be home. "So it looks like Stu and Maggie—that's their names—got away again."

Just then, Terry came out of the bathroom. Apparently, he had overheard some of their conversation and asked, "The detective was here? Looking for *me?*"

"Don't worry," Annette reassured him. "I only told him about Ruby and Uncle Will. He doesn't know *you* were here."

"Hmm." Terry frowned and wandered into the living room to join the others, who were fussing over the decorations on the Christmas tree.

"Here, Annette, take some of these cookies and fudge in for the others." Mrs. Vetter piled decorated sugar cookies, coconut balls and chocolate fudge onto a Santa Claus plate that was on the counter. "I'll have some hot milk ready soon for cocoa. Then I'll warm up the rest of that chili. Do we have enough?"

Annette checked the refrigerator and nodded at her mother. "Don't forget to call the hospital," she said as she carried the plate of goodies into the living room.

Tim took Annette aside after he'd snatched a cookie off the plate that was being passed around. "Hey, I've got to get home and help Dad with the milking."

"Sure," said Annette. "Thanks for all your help, Tim." She smiled up at him.

Terry interrupted them. "Let me come with you," he said to Tim. "Maybe I can help you in the milking parlor. I did gain a little experience working at the Randts', you know. You probably could use a hand."

Tim shrugged. "Sure, why not? Come on." He then called to his sister. "Penny ... one of us will come back and get you in about an hour. That okay?"

Penny nodded her head eagerly. Annette was relieved, too, that Penny was going to stick around. Her friend had already put some Christmas records on and the house was filled with the voice of Andy Williams singing *O Little Town of Bethlehem*. She knew it would help everyone settle down after the excitement of the day.

Mrs. Vetter was just hanging up the phone when Annette followed the boys through the kitchen. They put on their coats and left, and Annette turned to her mother. "Do you have to go in tonight?"

"No," said Mrs. Vetter with a relieved smile. "They're not busy at all. I told them I'd be on standby."

"I'm so glad," said Annette. "Mom, Ruby can sleep up in my room. Maybe Uncle Will can sleep down here on the couch ... or maybe Terry wants the couch and Uncle Will can have the spare room."

"Then help me put clean sheets on the bed," said Mrs. Vetter. "I think I've got time before the water gets hot." She led the way up the stairs and Annette followed.

While they got the guest room ready, Mrs. Vetter told Annette how Ruby had directed them to the cabin where her uncle had been waiting. To their relief, the Duncans' four-wheel-drive truck had been able to get through the snowy lanes which the snow plows hadn't yet reached.

She said that when they arrived at the cabin, they found Uncle Will inside, still in pain, but glad that help had finally come. He hadn't been able to bring in any more firewood and the fire had gone out, leaving only coals.

"I wrapped his knee with an Ace bandage I brought along," explained her mother, "and then I gave him some aspirin before we helped him out to the truck. Ruby got her things and some of his clothes. I'm afraid his station wagon is stuck until someone can get over there to dig it out."

"Well, thank goodness you hadn't left for work yet," said Annette.

"Yes, it would have been a hardship for EMTs to get in there." Mrs. Vetter pulled off the old bedding and threw it on the floor next to the door.

Annette lifted the fresh set of sheets out of a dresser drawer and her eyes fell on the file box that was still in the corner. "Mom, did you take that folder out of the box? You know, the one about Dad's first marriage."

Her mother took the folded bundle of white cotton sheets and separated the pillowcases. "Yes, I did," she admitted. "I had been into that box last weekend after Terry tried to call me at the hospital."

"But you didn't talk to him?"

"No, certainly not," said Mrs. Vetter. She shook the bottom sheet and laid it over the mattress pad. "But he had given the name Knutson. I went to the file box to check on the name."

Annette grabbed the pillows and pulled the case over the first one. "Where's the file now?"

"I have it in my room." Then, as if to purposely change the subject, her mother said, "Tim told me about the new calf."

"Yes, we have a little bullock." Annette helped smooth the bottom sheet as her mom tucked in the ends.

"Have you thought of a name for him yet?"

"Well, no," said Annette. "Since Mr. Duncan is going to take him after the first of the year anyway, I didn't think we should bother to name him."

"You're probably right, dear."

"Oops, I think I hear the tea kettle," said Annette. "I'll finish this, Mom."

Mrs. Vetter left the bed-making chore to her daughter,

and hurried downstairs to fix everybody a hot drink.

As soon as Annette was satisfied with the spare bedroom, she peeked into her own room quickly and made sure she had made up her bed that morning. Then she remembered that there was something in her purse that she needed. Downstairs, she could hear voices laughing and singing Christmas carols. She decided to take five minutes for herself, and found a roll of Christmas paper in her closet.

"Gee, maybe Pen and I *should* name the little calf," she said to herself as she reached for the Scotch tape on her small desk.

It was dark and cold outside later, when Annette finished checking her cows and had milked Elizabeth. After closing up the chickens, she carried a pocketful of eggs into the house, put them into the refrigerator, then took off her coat and joined the rest of them in the living room.

"Thank you, Helen, for the delicious supper," Uncle Will told Mrs. Vetter after they had eaten the left-over chili and some fruit salad. He was feeling better, Annette could tell, with his left leg propped up by a pillow on a hassock.

Ruby sat on the floor, petting Ginger, who lay on his side, soaking up all the attention, while Penny sat beside the younger girl, paging through a magazine. Once in a while, she would point to something on a page, and Ruby would giggle.

"I'm glad you're feeling better, Will," said Annette's mother, who sat on the other end of the couch and had picked up her knitting. Annette noticed that her mother looked fairly content, even under the circumstances. After all, the FBI was still searching for Terry, Ruby and Will Knutson. Yet this evening — Christmas Eve — her world was quiet and comfortable, at least for the moment. It did her heart good to see her mother happy, for a change.

"Tom was a good ranger," Will was telling her. "I

remember a lot of good times we had all those years ago." He smiled and took a sip of hot cocoa.

"I'm so sorry about your sister," said Mrs. Vetter. "Of course, I never met Ruth."

"Ruth had a lot of problems," said Will. "She had a drinking problem for one, but she licked that after Bob came into her life. He was a good influence on her ... oh, *not* that Tom wasn't." He cleared his throat. "It's just that ... I think she wasn't ready to settle down when she married Tom."

"So he told me," said Mrs. Vetter.

Annette studied her mother's face out of the corner of her eye. She still wondered why her mother had never bothered to tell her about her father having been married to Ruth Knutson. But it didn't really matter now.

Uncle Will and her mother continued to reminisce about the "good old days" and Annette joined Penny and Ruby on the floor underneath the Christmas tree. The twinkling, colored lights were mesmerizing, and Annette yawned and stretched.

"I'm getting tired too," said Ruby. "Where am I going to sleep tonight?"

"You can sleep up in my room," said Annette. "Do you want to?"

Ruby smiled shyly. "I don't want to be a bother."

"You're not," Annette insisted.

Ruby grinned. "Okay. Does Ginger sleep up there too?"

"He does," said Annette. At the mention of his name, the collie lifted his head and licked Ruby's hand. "He always sleeps on the rug next to my bed."

"I just love Ginger," said Ruby and put her arms around the dog.

Penny stood up and stretched. "Gee, it's getting late. I've got to be getting home. Tomorrow is Christmas. Annette, I wonder why Tim hasn't come to get me."

"I dunno, Pen. Why don't you give him a call?"

Penny went into the dining room, where the telephone was, and called the Duncan farm. Annette and Ruby petted Ginger and felt soothed by the records playing softly, bringing the magical air of the holiday into their hearts and minds. Annette, too, was wondering what was taking Tim and Terry so long. She had expected them to return half an hour ago.

After a few minutes, Penny came back into the living room. "Tim said he sent Terry over here with the truck about forty-five minutes ago."

Annette got up off the floor and beckoned to Penny to talk with her in the kitchen, where they could be alone. *"What?"* she said. "Where is Terry?"

"Well, I don't know," said Penny. "I told Tim to come and get me with the Chevelle."

Annette went and turned on the back porch light, but only the Vetters' car was in the driveway. There was no sign of the Duncans' truck ... nor Terry.

Suddenly, the phone rang, and both girls gasped. Annette ran into the dining room, eager to answer it.

"Hello, Annette, this is Bob Brennan," said the voice.

Annette's heart suddenly pounded. She was caught off guard. "Y-yes?"

"Annette, has your mother returned yet with Will Knutson and Ruby Foley? Since you didn't call, I thought I'd better give you a ring." His tone sounded serious and Annette swallowed.

"Uh ..." She was going to fib to him, but then she decided she needed to tell him the truth. "Actually, Detective ... they are here."

"They are?"

"Yes," admitted Annette. "Tim Duncan brought them back, with my mom, not long ago. Mr. Knutson's knee is sprained and Mom treated him."

"Do you need an ambulance?"

"No!" cried Annette. "Everything's fine. He's resting … and-and… Ruby's fine, too."

"And what about Terry Knutson?" demanded the detective.

"No … No, Terry's not here," Annette affirmed. She then moved as far from the living room entrance as the cord would stretch, so that no one in there could hear. "Please, Detective Brennan … please don't come and arrest anyone tonight. It's Christmas Eve."

Bob Brennan cleared his throat. "Don't worry, Annette, I'm not going to come out and arrest anyone tonight. After all, as you said, it *is* Christmas Eve." He cleared his throat again, then said, "It sounds to me like you've got things pretty much under control." Then he added, "Plus, I'm positive that Mr. Chase, that FBI agent, isn't going to want to disrupt his family holiday in Madison to drive back up here tonight."

Annette sighed with gratitude. "Thanks … Bob." It felt awkward calling the detective by his first name. Penny, next to her, giggled. Then Annette asked, "Did you go and talk to Mr. Brown this afternoon about those two hippies?"

Detective Brennan then revealed that, after he had dropped off Annette and Penny that afternoon, he had stopped at Browns' Store. "I got to him just as he was closing up early … being Christmas Eve and all. And it's a good thing, too. He not only remembered those two … Stu and Maggie … but he complained that they were rude to his customers and they came in once or twice every day … and he mentioned that she would always go straight into that restroom … without fail."

Annette recalled that time Maggie had charged out of the restroom and almost run over her.

"So … Mr. Brown and I went into the restroom and had a look around. And you'll never guess." He paused, then said, "We found a hole in the wall behind the commode that was covered with a rag. Inside that, there were packets of marijuana and some drugs."

"Wow!" exclaimed Annette.

Penny was motioning to her. "What? What?"

"We think we have enough evidence now to arrest those two," said Detective Brennan. "Also, Mr. Brown saw something slip to the floor from underneath Miss Maggie's coat the last time they were in. He said the FBI agent was there, flashing his badge, and those two high-tailed it out of there."

Annette couldn't help smiling as she pictured the scene in her mind.

"That's not all," said Detective Brennan. "There was a paper with some phone numbers on it in an envelope ... most likely contacts of customers that were buying the drugs from them. We sent a patrol car out to the farmhouse again this evening. But like before, nobody was there. The two of them seem to have fled."

Annette thanked Detective Brennan one more time for letting Ruby and Uncle Will have some peace on Christmas Eve. She didn't know what was going to happen the next day ... or the day after that ... but she knew that she needed more time. She had a nagging feeling that Terry might be on the run again.

Ten minutes later, Tim showed up to the Vetters'. Before he took Penny home, he asked Annette if he could go check on the new calf.

"Sure," said Annette. "I'll come with you." She called to Penny, who was talking with Ruby in the living room.

"Take your time," Penny called back to her. "That will give me time to say goodbye to Ruby and Uncle Will."

"Do you have to go?" Ruby had obviously grown fond of Penny.

Annette poked her head through the doorway and saw that her mom and Uncle Will were engrossed in tales of the olden days. She told her mom she was going to the barn and would be right back in, and Mrs. Vetter waved her off, laughing at one of Uncle Will's jokes.

As they walked outside together, Tim carrying a flashlight, he said, "Your mom and Will seem to be hitting it off."

"It seems that way," said Annette. She yawned again.

"Tired?" he asked.

"I didn't sleep much last night, and with all the excitement today ..."

He opened the barn door, then ushered her inside. They turned on the light and could see that everything was in order. Elizabeth was chewing her cud, and Alice was lying down on the straw, her baby cuddled up against her. The light had aroused them, and the calf's ears twitched.

"Aww ... he is so cute," said Annette.

"Are you going to name him?" asked Tim.

"Well, Penny and I talked about it after supper," said Annette. "We decided his name should be Donovan ... you know, like the singer." Tim gazed at her, so she added, "Like in ... they call me *Mellow Yellow*."

At that, Tim laughed.

"I know, I know ..." Annette sighed. "Your dad's gonna buy him off us. But he can have a name until he leaves in January."

Suddenly, she felt Tim's arm around her. She was very aware of his closeness. She turned her face to meet his. "Tim ... thanks again for helping me with Alice. You are so ... so good with animals."

Tim's green eyes had her under a spell, and the next thing she knew, he bent close and planted a kiss squarely on her mouth. She didn't resist. She closed her eyes and welcomed the warmth and the excitement that shot through her chest and made her heart race. He held the kiss for several seconds, and then slowly pulled away and smiled down at her.

Suddenly, the barn door flew open and Penny came

running in. She stopped the moment she saw the two of them clinging to each other. Penny's green eyes expanded and a big grin crossed her face. "I caught you! Ah-ha! I knew it all along."

Embarrassed, Annette turned away to compose herself. Tim wasn't embarrassed at all. He laughed at his sister. "What's that s'posed to mean? How come you came barging in here, anyway?"

"We ... we just came out to ... to check on Alice," said Annette in a meek voice.

Penny laughed. "Annette, why are you so *red?*"

"It's none of your business," Tim taunted his sister. "Come on, I'm taking you home. After all, it's past your bedtime, little sister."

As Penny turned to follow him out, she stopped and said, "Hey, what's this?"

Annette walked over to the barn door, where Penny pointed to a piece of note paper that was tacked to the wood on the inside. Tim turned around and came over to them. Penny grabbed the paper and pulled it down. "It's a note," she said. She was having trouble reading it in the dim light of the barn.

"Maybe it's from Terry." Annette snatched it from her friend.

Both Tim and Penny were astounded. Annette held the note up to the dim light and read it slowly out loud:

DEAR ANNETTE,

I HAD TO LEAVE FOR AWHILE. THERE IS SOMETHING I HAVE TO DO.

I WILL BE BACK TOMORROW. PLEASE TELL RUBY EVERYTHING IS ALL RIGHT. I AM MAKING SURE OF IT.

LOVE, YOUR BROTHER

Penny gasped and covered her mouth as she stared at Annette's face. Tim was equally surprised. Annette sighed and read the note to herself once more, then faced her friends.

"Is it true?" cried Penny.

"Terry is your *brother?*" asked Tim.

"Half brother," said Annette. "Terry's my half brother. I just found out last night."

"Oh, my gosh," breathed Penny. "So that's why ..."

"I thought there was some kind of resemblance between you two," said Tim.

"That's why you were so concerned about him," added Penny.

It took a minute for her friends to soak in the revelation.

"Well, at least he said he's coming back," Tim finally said. "That's good."

"Yeah, considering he has Dad's truck," said Penny.

Tim led Penny out the door. "Good night, Annette." He smiled at her.

"Don't forget ... you're all invited to come over for Christmas dinner at our house," Penny reminded her.

Annette turned off the light, then closed the barn door and followed her friends out to the Chevelle, with its engine still running. She waited until Tim and Penny were inside and had backed up to the road. Then she stuffed Terry's note into her pocket and stepped onto the back porch, pausing a moment before opening the door.

"He *kissed* me," she said to herself, a smile on her face. Then she went inside.

19

Christmas Morning

"Is it true, Annette?" Ruby, dressed in one of Annette's nightgowns, brushed her long blond hair in front of the mirror on Annette's dresser up in her bedroom. "Is Terry your brother too?"

Annette had just come into the room, dressed in her robe after brushing her teeth. She smiled and sat down on the bed. "Yes, I guess he is."

"Uncle Will told me, and that's what your mom said."

"Then it must be true," said Annette, fluffing Ruby's pillow for her.

"He said Terry's father was *your* father."

"Yes."

"And that your dad died." Ruby set the brush down and looked at Annette with sympathy in her eyes. "It's so awful, Annette. You lost your dad, and I lost both my ... my mom is gone too. *And* my dad."

"Well, Ruby ... I know it's really hard for you right now. But life is full of lots of blessings, too."

Ruby crawled into the bed beside Annette. "I know."

Annette turned off the light on her night stand. She could see the ray of light coming from the bedroom next to hers, where Uncle Will was spending the night. Her mother had already gone to bed and her door was shut.

"I have a lot to be thankful for." Ruby pulled the covers up to her neck. "Even though I don't have parents anymore, I have Terry ... and Uncle Will ... and ... and ... now I have you and Helen."

"What a kind thing to say," said Annette.

"At first, I was afraid when Terry took me to Uncle Will's trailer in Madison. He was a stranger to me. But soon I realized he was a good and kind man."

"Tell me what your dad was like." Annette settled herself under the covers.

"Well ... my dad is a hero," said Ruby. "He was in the Air Force and he flew bombers in Korea. In Vietnam he was a major. He could be a little strict at times, but he was a really good dad. I miss him so much." She sniffled.

"We don't have to talk about him, if you don't want to," Annette said softly.

"No, it helps when I talk about things out loud," said Ruby. She looked at the older girl. "Don't you think it helps when you can talk things out to someone?"

Annette nodded. She waited for Ruby to say more.

"I think that if I talk everything out, then I'll be able to go to sleep. I wasn't able to talk about what happened at the Yateses' until now. It was ... horrible."

"Were your foster parents mean to you?" asked Annette.

"No. Well, not at first." Ruby sighed. "Colonel Yates was super nice ... at the beginning. He gave me gifts and candy, and would take me shopping and buy me things."

"You and Mrs. Yates?" asked Annette.

"No, she'd stay home."

"Oh," said Annette.

"Betty ... that's Mrs. Yates ... was really quiet. She was afraid of the Colonel, I think. When he was with me, Betty would disappear into the bedroom and shut the door. She didn't want to see what was going on."

"And what was that?" Annette was almost afraid to ask after what Terry had told her.

"Colonel Yates wanted to play kissing games." She scrunched up her face. "*Yuck* ... it was quite disgusting, as you can imagine."

"Did he make you do things you didn't want to do?"

Ruby sighed again. "He'd promise me things that I wanted, but only if I would kiss him ... or let him fondle me ... you know, hug me ... only he did it ... he did it places that were private. I didn't like that. And I told him not to do that to me."

"Did it happen when you were alone with him?" asked Annette.

"Kind of. He didn't seem to care if Betty was in the other room. Then he started molesting me."

"Well, did you tell Betty?" asked Annette.

"Yes, but ... Betty looked the other way." Tears began to well up in Ruby's eyes. "She just said ... she said ... not to ... not to worry about it." A sob escaped her voice.

Annette felt herself growing angry. "Well, did you tell the social workers?"

"*Yes,*" Ruby insisted. "But no one ever believed me. And Betty ... Mrs. Yates ... always told a different side of the story. She would always back him up. Annette, no one at Social Services believed that the Colonel was a dirty old man who did nasty things to the girls they fostered."

"He did this to others?"

"Yes, what did you think?" Ruby was getting worked up.

"Oh, Ruby ... I'm so sorry about this."

"When Terry came that night to see me ... he and his friend, Charlie ... he caught Colonel Yates trying to hurt me. He wasn't expecting Terry's visit, and when Terry saw how I was crying and trying to get away from the Colonel, that's when Terry lost his temper. He started hitting him and yelling at him."

Annette could feel goose bumps erupting on her skin, just listening to Ruby's story.

"Betty came out of her bedroom and saw them fighting. She had a baseball bat. She wouldn't even call the police. She told Terry to get out. He told them he was taking me away, but *she* tried to stop him. Then, the Colonel jumped on Terry and they rolled around on the floor. The next thing I knew, Terry had grabbed a heavy jar ... or vase ... whatever it was on a nearby shelf ... and he struck Colonel Yates on the head.

"We thought he was dead, Annette. I was so scared ... not so much for myself as I was for Terry. Anyway, while Betty was crying over him on the floor ... getting all hysterical ... Terry took me and we split. Charlie was waiting out in his car and drove us back over to his house."

"Then what happened?" asked Annette.

"Well, Charlie's parents weren't home. Terry said he had to get us as far away as possible. He asked Charlie to give him some money — which he did — and then his friend, Jason, drove us up to Denver, where we got on the bus. And you know the rest. Terry called Uncle Will along the way, and he said we could stay there with him."

Annette got out of bed and grabbed the box of Kleenexes on her dresser for Ruby, who was still sniffling.

"But after we got to Madison, Terry never told me why he was going to Ravensville," Ruby continued, wiping her nose. "Uncle Will must have known Terry was looking for his dad. But he didn't tell *me* he was looking for his dad. I only found out today that Tom Vetter was my brother's father."

"Well, I'm glad Terry found us," said Annette. "And I'm glad you're here with us now, Ruby."

"Oh, so am I." She cried a little more. "So am *I*, Annette. And I'm so happy that Terry's going to be back tomorrow, like he wrote in the note."

Annette didn't reveal her feelings of doubt or her suspicion that Terry was running away to avoid the authorities. "What do you think is going to happen next?" she asked.

"I'm afraid to answer that," said Ruby, "or even to think about it." Then she snuggled onto her side. "I wish ... I wish you could be my sister too, Annette."

"We *are* sisters ... well, maybe not blood sisters, Ruby ... but we share the same brother, don't we?"

"That's right, we do! Oh, Annette, will you please ask your mom to adopt me?"

This took Annette by surprise. "Don't you want to stay with your uncle?" asked Annette.

"Uncle Will's very nice, but I like it here. I love it here in the country. I love your house. I love your bedroom. And I love Ginger ... and your mom. I want to be part of your family ... and Terry, too, of course." Then she added, "And Uncle Will's trailer is way too small for us. Plus he said he's a loner."

Annette couldn't help but laugh. Then she grew worried. She knew that Sam Chase, the FBI agent, and Bob Brennan would be out tomorrow or the next day, and then this fantasy of being part of a real family would be over.

But for just tonight ... on this beautiful, fantastic Christmas Eve ... she fell asleep, captivated with the idea that just maybe her wish was coming true. She could envision them as a family ... her mom, Terry, herself and Ruby ... one happy little family living on Ogden Road in Ravensville, Wisconsin.

Christmas morning arrived with more sunshine. Annette got up and tried to stay quiet, so as not to waken Ruby. The younger girl had tossed and turned in her sleep throughout the night. After what she had been through, who could blame her? Annette quickly dressed, and then Ginger went with her downstairs and out to the barn to milk Elizabeth.

"Good morning, Donovan," Annette called when she saw the new baby bullock standing next to Alice. His big black ears perked up at the sight of her, and Alice answered with a soft "mooo."

While she milked Elizabeth, Annette recalled last night, when Tim had kissed her here in the barn. Maybe it hadn't been the most romantic place to be kissed, but she would never forget it. Tim had been her "secret love" for many months now. She had admired him for years, but it was only in the last year that he had started paying attention to her in a special new way. She knew he could have any girl that he wanted — and he often *did* — but she told herself she couldn't have expectations just because of what had happened. No, the two of them must carry on just as they always had.

But it was strange, she thought, that her crush on Pete Randt had dwindled. Remembering back to last Friday afternoon, when she had sat with Pete in the school auditorium, watching the Christmas pageant, Pete had actually held her hand … yet the whole time, she knew he had been focused on Penny. And that was absolutely fine with her now … she had *no qualms*. If Penny didn't believe her, she certainly must now that she had found Annette in her brother's embrace.

Later, when Annette returned to the house after doing the chores, her mother and Uncle Will were already up, drinking coffee in the kitchen. Ruby was upstairs taking a shower. They were relieved that Will's knee was doing better. He used a ski pole to help him walk. Mrs. Vetter had found it in one of the closets upstairs.

Her mother made a breakfast of bacon, eggs and waffles, which they ate in the dining room when Ruby came downstairs, wearing a set of clean jeans and a T-shirt from Annette's closet.

"Merry Christmas, Ruby," Mrs. Vetter greeted the girl.

"Oh, I'm so happy," said Ruby. She came over and gave

her uncle a hug, then Mrs. Vetter, and finally Annette too. "I was so afraid Christmas was going to be a disaster this year."

They ate breakfast, then went into the living room. Annette saw that her mother had put a few more colorfully wrapped gifts under the tree. Among them was the one little box in gold wrapping paper that Annette had put there last night before going to bed. It had Ruby's name on it.

"There's one for *me!*" the girl cried out in delight when she saw it.

"I'll be danged ... there *is* a St. Nicholas," chuckled Uncle Will.

"Well, Annette, I know you're anxious," said Mrs. Vetter. "Go ahead and open your presents."

Annette was a trifle embarrassed, being the one with the most presents under the tree. But nobody seemed offended. She opened the first two. One was a box with three pairs of new pantyhose. The next one was some stationery. "Thanks, Mom," she said. She decided to wait and open the rest later.

"Here, Ruby." Annette took the gold present out from under the tree. "This is for you."

"Not yet," said Ruby. "Helen? Aren't you going to open yours?"

"Oh yeah," said Annette. She found her present to her mother and handed it over.

Mrs. Vetter was delighted with the music box and fussed over it while Annette watched Ruby slowly take the wrapping off the little box.

"*Ohh!!*" Ruby's expression of joy was unparalleled. She held up the glass Christmas tree ornament with the ruby rhinestone at the top. It was the ornament she had admired at the gas station on the edge of town, when Annette had seen her for the first time. Jimmy, the gas station attendant, had sold it to her for less than the asking price. "Oh, Annette, thank you! I love it so much." She hugged it to her breast.

Just then, they heard a knock on the back door. Ginger jumped up from his place at Uncle Will's feet and barked.

"Terry!" Annette and Ruby yelled together. Both of them were on their feet in a flash and ran through the dining room, into the kitchen.

But when they opened the door, it wasn't Terry. Instead, Tim and Penny stood on the porch with an armload of presents. Penny was grinning from ear to ear as they came inside and carried the bundle of presents into the Vetters' living room.

"What? Really?" Annette was so surprised, and only a trifle disappointed because it hadn't been Terry.

"Mom and Dad had some extra gifts stashed," Tim said in Annette's ear. "They're for your guests."

"How wonderful," marveled Mrs. Vetter when the Duncans brought in the presents and set them down. For the next few minutes, they watched as Ruby and Uncle Will opened a couple of gifts each, and then Penny stuck one for Terry under the Christmas tree.

"We can't really stay," Tim told the rest. "But you're coming for dinner, aren't you?"

Mrs. Vetter sighed. "Well, the rest of them are. I'm afraid I have to go in to work today."

"Aww, Mom ..." Annette moaned.

"It'll be okay, dear," Mrs. Vetter replied cheerfully. "You all go and enjoy dinner at the Duncans'."

Penny took Annette aside before she and Tim left. "He hasn't shown up yet?" she asked in reference to Terry.

Annette shook her head.

"Annette, what if he doesn't ... come back, I mean?"

"Pen, he's *got* to."

"Well, where do you think he went?"

"I have no idea."

Tim came over to them and said, "Dad's fit to be tied about the truck situation. You know, he could report this to the sheriff. It's only because we begged him not to."

Annette sighed with frustration and worry. "I'm sure Terry would not have taken the truck unless he had a good reason. We've got to give him the benefit of a doubt."

"I don't like this," muttered Tim. "Come on, Pen."

"We'll see you at two." Penny called over Annette's shoulder. "Bye, Ruby."

"Thanks, Penny," the girl called from the living room.

That afternoon, Mrs. Vetter drove Annette, Ruby and Uncle Will over to the Duncan farm. She was on her way to work at the hospital and felt she absolutely had an obligation to be there on Christmas Day. When they arrived at the Duncans', Audrey Duncan came out of the farmhouse carrying a brown bag, which she handed to Annette's mother through the car window.

"We're sorry you won't be joining us, Helen," said Mrs. Duncan. "I put some turkey, stuffing and some fresh-baked rolls and a piece of pumpkin pie in here for you to enjoy."

"Bless your heart, Audrey." Annette's mother reached her gloved hand out to Mrs. Duncan and they chatted for a moment while Annette and Ruby helped Uncle Will get out of the front seat. As soon as introductions were finished, Mrs. Vetter drove off and everybody else went into the house.

Ruby fell in love with Penny's dog, The Cheeze, and was becoming acquainted with the youngest member of the family, 6-year-old Karen. Penny stayed in the kitchen, helping her mother, while Annette stared out the front window at the big red dairy barn across the wide lawn. She had left a written note on the door back home, explaining where they were, in case Terry returned. She was growing more and more worried about him. *Where was he?*

They were just getting ready to sit down to dinner when the telephone rang. When Mrs. Duncan called to Annette, she hurried to answer it, thinking maybe it was Terry. Instead, she was greeted by Bob Brennan.

"I was going to wait and call you later," said the detective, "but I wanted you to know that the sheriff picked up Maggie and Stu around noon today. They were arrested out at the ranger hut next to the old tower, where they must have spent the night."

"Oh, wow…" said Annette.

Detective Brennan continued, "They received an anonymous tip from a man this morning. Otherwise they might not have been caught."

Annette had a suspicion that Terry had been the one who gave the anonymous tip, but she didn't dare say anything. She thanked Bob Brennan for calling her, then hung up and took Penny aside to tell her the news.

"Oh, what a relief," said Penny.

"I just wish I knew where he called from," said Annette.

"You and me both."

They sat down to their meal of roast turkey, mashed potatoes and gravy, cranberry sauce, squash and green beans, along with homemade dinner rolls. Annette sat with Ruby on her right and Penny on her left. Tim sat across from her and whenever their eyes would meet, he would smile at her in his dazzling way.

Uncle Will was enjoying his visit with Ray Duncan, and Audrey was fussing over Karen's needs and kept getting up to bring things from the kitchen.

The phone rang while Annette was almost finished. It was for Penny, but after a minute, she came back to the table and told Annette that Pete had called. "He wants to talk to you," she said.

Annette wiped her mouth with a napkin, then got up and went into the Duncans' kitchen. Penny hovered close while Annette picked up the receiver. "Hi, Pete."

"Merry Christmas," said Pete.

"Merry Christmas to you too," she said.

"Annette, I thought you should know. Terry came back."

Annette gasped. "When?"

"He showed up this morning."

"Thank goodness!"

"Wait," said Pete. "He took off again."

"Oh, no," said Annette.

Pete sighed. "Penny explained to me how Terry showed up at your place. She told me you're related to him. Are you really?"

"Yes, Pete. He's my half brother."

"Hey, that's groovy. Who'd ever have thought?"

"Pete, did Terry say where he was headed?"

"No. Actually, he just showed up here and said he needed to get some stuff he'd left behind. Mom made him eat something. Then he just … took off."

"Pete! I have to know where he went," cried Annette. "What else did he tell you?"

"All he said was he had to get away. He said he had to leave town. He didn't want to get anybody in trouble."

"Did he have the truck?" Penny asked, trying to talk into the phone at the same time.

Annette repeated to Pete what Penny had asked.

"Truck? There wasn't any truck," said Pete.

"The Duncans' black truck," Annette clarified. "Terry had it yesterday."

"No, I thought he was on foot," said Pete. "But he might have parked it on the road."

Annette was close to tears and handed the phone to Penny. "Here, you talk to him. I … I can't …" She ran into the bathroom to cry. She couldn't believe that Terry had run away again, that he had lost the Duncans' truck, and that she was never going to see her brother again.

After a couple of minutes, someone knocked on the bathroom door. "Annette." It was Tim. "Is everything okay in there?"

Annette opened the door a crack and peered out at him with her tear-stained face.

"Hey … what's wrong?"

"Tim, I'm so worried. We've got to find Terry."

Tim stepped inside the bathroom and closed the door. "You've been crying." He put his arms around her and she welcomed his embrace. It was such a comfort to lean against him. Then he gently pulled away and smiled at her. "Okay. Tell you what. As soon as we're done eating, I'll help you look for him. What did Pete say?"

Annette repeated all that she knew, which wasn't much. They were both very concerned that now the Duncans' truck was missing.

"Where are you going?" called Mrs. Duncan when Tim and Annette got on their coats and headed for the door. Dinner was over and Ruby was helping Karen clear the table.

"I've got to help Annette with something," Tim explained. "Pen … can you come?"

Penny wasn't about to miss out. She grabbed her coat and mittens, then the three of them hurried out to Tim's Chevelle. The girls climbed into the back seat and Tim started up the engine.

"You know, if we can't find him … Dad's gonna have to call the sheriff," Penny told Annette.

"I know." She sniffed. "I know that." She swallowed. She hadn't felt like having any pumpkin pie.

They drove past the Vetter farmhouse, then drove out to the Randt farm on Gaston Road. The girls looked on either side of the road as Tim drove slowly, looking for any sign of a pedestrian or the truck that might have been left alongside the road. Finally, Annette directed Tim to go to that spot where the path went through the woods to the ranger hut near the old tower.

"That's where the sheriff arrested those two hippies," she said. "I think we should check that hut out."

"I can't drive in there with my car," said Tim.

"We can walk," said Penny.

"It's not too far in," said Annette. "Less than a mile."

Tim parked the car when they got to the clearing off the side of the road. It looked like the snow had been trampled a lot more, and there was still evidence left from Terry's wood-cutting job for Mr. Brown. After Tim locked the car, the three of them plodded through the woods, determined to reach the hut before it started getting dark.

They were cold and worn out by the time they reached the tower and the ramshackle hut beside it. When they stepped inside the dilapidated building, they could see that it had been cleaned out completely. The blanket, the crates and litter were all gone. There were obvious signs of a skirmish, with lots of footprints in the snow. This was where Maggie and Stu had been caught and arrested by the sheriff's deputies. She wondered if Terry had been hiding out nearby. How else would he have known Maggie and Stu were there?

"It's getting dark," said Tim. "We'd better get back to the car."

"He's gone, Annette," said Penny sadly.

Taking a deep breath, Annette said nothing, but led the other two back through the woods toward the waiting Chevelle.

20

A Dream Come True

When Tim pulled into the Duncans' driveway at dusk, the three of them saw two cars parked next to the porch. One of them Annette recognized as Bob Brennan's sedan. The other car was white and had government plates. "Oh, no," groaned Annette.

"Detective Brennan's here," Penny told Tim.

"And I think the FBI guy is here as well," said Annette.

"Wait!" cried Tim as he came to a stop next to an outbuilding. He pointed toward the barn. "Look ... it's the truck."

"Oh, my gosh," cried Penny.

Annette could see the Duncans' old four-wheel-drive black pickup parked over by the barn. "Terry must be here," she assumed. "Hurry up and let me out."

All three of them were in a rush to get inside the house. They found the Duncan family seated in the large living room. Uncle Will and Ruby sat together on the loveseat sofa, facing the two law enforcement men, who were conversing with them. Annette could see no sign of Terry.

"They're here now," said Audrey Duncan.

"Hello, Mr. Brennan," said Penny.

Bob Brennan stood up, along with the large FBI man, who

was dressed casually in sweat pants and a heavy sweater. "Sam, this is Annette Vetter, Tim and Penny Duncan."

Annette took her turn shaking the FBI agent's hand, then gazed at Ruby and Uncle Will. Ruby clung to Will and seemed on edge.

"Where's Terry?" asked Tim. "The truck's back."

"Yes, but we don't know when," said Ray Duncan.

"Nobody saw it drive in," added Audrey Duncan.

"I checked the barn, but couldn't find him," said Ray.

"So ... Terry's not here?" Annette murmured.

Everyone seated shook their heads no.

"That must mean you did not find him either," said Detective Brennan. "We all assume that's where you kids went ... looking for the kid."

Tim explained how they had driven around after hearing that Terry had stopped at the Randt farm that morning. "We went to the old tower, but no one was there," he explained.

"Are you going to arrest him when you find him?" Annette was trembling.

Bob Brennan glanced at Sam Chase, and the FBI agent stepped forward. "No, Miss Vetter. We have no intention of taking the young Knutson fellow into custody. The charges against him have been cleared. We simply needed to hear Ruby's story to verify what happened in Colorado Springs."

"So, Colonel Yates is alive and well?" she asked.

"He suffered a skull fracture," said the FBI agent. "His wife accused Terry Knutson of aggravated assault. But since that wasn't the case, and he was only defending his sister, Terry was wanted only for transporting a minor across state lines. And, as it turned out, some other girls came forward after they heard about the incident, and Colonel Yates has been charged with child endangerment and sex crimes related to the foster care in their home."

Ruby buried her head in her hands and cried. Uncle Will

pulled her close to him, which seemed to comfort the girl.

"Oh, what a relief." Penny grinned and hugged Annette. "Terry's off the hook."

"Yes, he's not wanted for murder ... in any degree," said Bob Brennan. "However ..." He looked at the FBI agent. "Sam, you tell them."

After clearing his throat, the FBI agent said, "We still have the matter of Ruby Foley," he said.

Ruby looked up and dabbed at her eyes at the mention of her name. She shot Annette a pleading look. "What?" she asked innocently.

"Both you and your brother are minors," said Sam Chase. "I need to take you back to Colorado for the State to decide what legal action they need to take, since you have no one to be your guardian."

Uncle Will raised his hand then. "I will offer to give them a home," he said. "I'm Ruby's only living relative."

"*No*, Uncle Will." Ruby shook her head. "I can't stay with you." She looked at Annette. "I'm going to be Annette's sister. Terry and I are going to stay in Ravensville with Helen and Annette."

Everyone in the room looked at Annette, who had blushed in embarrassment, but then smiled. "That's right. Ruby and I talked about it. And I'm going to have a talk with my mother tonight."

"Terry is Annette's half brother," announced Ruby. "It only makes sense that we stick together as a family." The blond girl managed a smile for the first time since the two men had come to the house and disrupted her happiness on Christmas.

"Is that right?" Bob Brennan's eyebrows shot up as he glanced at Annette. "Your brother?"

"His name should actually be Terry Vetter," said Annette. "My dad's name is on his birth certificate."

"Well, I'm sure that if Mrs. Vetter motions the court, it

should be a pretty open-and-shut case," said Sam Chase. "But first ... you need to find Terry Knutson."

"Terry said he'd be back today," said Ruby. "He promised."

The two men headed for the door. "This has been quite a day," said Sam Chase.

Detective Brennan patted the agent on the back. "Why don't you come on over to my house for the night? You can drive back to Madison tomorrow ... after we know Knutson has shown up."

"All right," said the agent. "Man, I could use a Tom and Jerry on a night like this."

"Tess can make us one at home." Bob Brennan turned to Annette and said, "Call me."

"Okay," she agreed.

"I mean it, Annette." He winked.

Ruby jumped up from the couch and ran to Annette and threw her arms around her. "Everything's going to be all right, Annette. We're going to be a family!"

"I sure hope so, Ruby." Annette sighed as she hugged her new little sister. "I really truly hope so."

"Will? How do you feel about all this?" asked Ray Duncan.

Uncle Will shrugged, and then a silly smile spread over his face. "It makes no difference to me."

"Oh, Uncle Will, I'm sorry if I hurt your feelings," said Ruby, turning back to her uncle. "I love you too. I really do. But Annette's house is much better for us. Your trailer's kinda ... close quarters."

Everyone laughed at that.

Then, Annette glanced outside to see the two sets of head-lights as the two vehicles backed out toward the road. She turned to Penny and Tim and said, "I'm going to run home. I have to milk Elizabeth. It's getting late. Please call me if Terry shows up."

"We certainly will," said Tim.

"At least he brought the truck back," called out their father.

"Want us to go with you?" asked Penny.

"No, thanks. I need some alone time … to think," she replied with a quick smile.

Annette borrowed a flashlight from the Duncans' and walked the quarter mile down the road to the Vetter farmhouse. The night air was nippy, but the sky was clear with bright stars shining up high. Bare-branched trees shrouded both sides of Ogden Road.

The house was dark, but Annette could hear Ginger barking from inside the porch. She called to him. "It's me, boy!" As soon as she reached the porch, where he had been confined when they had all gone to the Duncans' for dinner, the collie greeted her in his usual enthusiastic manner. Together, they walked straight to the barn.

Annette was surprised to find the light on inside. She must have forgotten to turn it off that morning. Elizabeth was waiting, with a full udder, to be milked, and Alice and the bullock were together in the stall.

"Hi, Annette."

At the sound of Terry's voice, Annette jumped and saw the tall blond boy in his green parka crouched in the corner beside the equipment room. "Terry!" She grinned with excitement. "Oh, am I ever glad to see *you.*"

"I promised I'd be back," he said. "I see you got my note." He stood and stretched.

"I sure did! Oh, Terry … so much has happened."

"Yes," he said. "I wanted to see you again before I … before I have to go away again."

"*Go away?*" Annette was stunned. "What do you mean? You can't leave now."

"I'm afraid I have to, Annette. I know that the FBI is hot on my trail." He sighed. "That's why I'm here, Annette. I'm tired of running. I'm ready to give up and go to the police. It's time that I face whatever is ahead of me in Colorado."

"But, Terry, you've been *cleared*."

Elizabeth mooed loudly, as if to remind Annette of her delayed chore.

Terry tilted his head and wore a puzzled frown. "Huh? What are you talking about?"

Annette went into the equipment room and retrieved her milking pail and a rag, then came out and walked over to the cow. Terry stood behind her, his hands still in his pockets.

"Sam Chase, the FBI agent, and Bob Brennan were over at the Duncans' just a while ago," she told him. "They were talking to your Uncle Will and to Ruby." She sat on the milking stool and cleaned Elizabeth's teats while she explained to her brother what the law enforcement men had revealed about the Yateses.

"Annette, if it's true ... but how *can* I believe it's true?"

"It's true, Terry. I *swear* it." She looked up at him as her fingers worked away and the milk started shooting into the metal pail.

"Then ... this means ..."

"Yes!" Annette grinned up at him. "Terry, you're free. You don't have to run anymore."

After the milking was done and she had checked to see that the chickens were okay, Annette and Terry went to the house, Ginger trotting behind them. She turned on the lights and, without even taking her coat off first, went to the telephone and dialed the Duncans' number.

Twenty minutes later, Tim and Penny arrived in the Chevelle with Uncle Will and Ruby, and there was a jubilant reunion as the three family members hugged each other and cried a little. Annette made some hot chocolate while Penny went into the living room to turn on the Christmas lights. With the tree lit up, she put on some Christmas music. Tim lingered in the kitchen to help Annette.

"Your mom called from the hospital after you came over here," Tim told her. "She's coming home early tonight."

Annette was elated at the news as she heated milk on the stove. "Oh, that's fantastic."

"Got any marshmallows?" he asked.

"Up on that top shelf of the cupboard," Annette directed. She was measuring cocoa into each mug and reached for the sugar bowl and the salt shaker.

"Do you think your mom will take in Terry and Ruby?" he asked.

"I really hope so, Tim." Then she squinted at him. "Do you think she'll have a problem with that? I mean, getting a coupl'a more kids is a lot more responsibility."

"Do ya think?" He gave her a playful pinch. "I think the more, the merrier." She caught his look and then froze as Tim reached down and pecked her on the cheek.

"Whoa-ho! I saw that." Penny had walked into the kitchen and witnessed the kiss.

"Why are you always in the right place at the wrong time?" hollered Tim. He reached into the cupboard for the bag of marshmallows.

"Annette, do you seriously *like* that big lug?" Penny had her hands on her hips, but a smile was on her face.

Terry popped in behind Penny. "What lug?" he asked, looking around.

They all laughed. After the hot cocoa was ready, Tim helped Annette carry the mugs into the living room to the others. Penny had brought out Terry's present, which she had placed under the Christmas tree that morning.

"Something for me?" He smiled as he accepted the large,

rather flat package.

"Well ... yeah," she said. "I hope you like it. It was really supposed to be for Annette."

"You're not supposed to say *that*," Tim chided her.

"What?" Annette looked surprised. "For me?"

"Here ..." Terry tried to hand the package to her, but she waved her hands at him.

"Open it, Terry." Ruby was smiling with excitement.

Terry slowly unwrapped the green paper and opened the box. Then he stared at what was inside and grinned. Turning to Annette, he pulled out a record album, and all the girls in the room screamed out, "*Cream!!!*"

Uncle Will put his hands over his ears. "What the heck *is* that?"

"Thank you, Penny. And thank you, Tim." Terry turned the album over. "I'm going to share it with everyone."

"Put it on now," begged Ruby.

"But Christmas music is playing," objected Penny.

"Take it off. Put on the Cream," insisted Annette.

Rock and roll was playing at high volume several minutes later when Mrs. Vetter came home and walked in to see everyone having a good time in the living room. She smiled and set her knitting basket down, then removed her coat. She and Uncle Will exchanged looks that said to each other, *How long do we have to put up with this?*

"I have a present for Uncle Will," said Terry after the music had ended. The room had quieted down. Mrs. Vetter had fixed herself a glass of milk and was passing around the plate of fudge and cookies when the blond boy stood up to address them. "Your station wagon is at Browns' Store."

"What?" Annette stared in surprise.

"My station wagon?" Uncle Will's eyebrows shot up.

"You dug it out at the cabin?" asked Ruby.

"How did you know where to find my car?" Uncle Will

was mystified.

Terry explained. "After I went to the Randts' house this morning, to get my things, I was walking to the Duncans' truck, which I had parked off the highway before I got there. Well, I had just started going down the road to come back here ... when this man came hiking out of that side road. He saw me and came over and asked if I could use the truck to help him get his vehicle started. He said he was staying at one of the cabins in the woods, and the car wouldn't start. He needed a jump."

Annette and Penny looked at one another. "What side road?" Penny asked.

"Was there a green farmhouse?" asked Annette.

"I think so," said Terry. "Not too far off the road."

"That was where Maggie and Stu lived," Annette told her mother.

"Who are Maggie and Stu?" asked Mrs. Vetter.

"Those hippies that tried to drug me with their tea," cried Ruby. "The ones I ran away from when Tim and Penny drove by."

"Oh, that's right." Mrs. Vetter sipped her glass of milk.

"The sheriff's deputies arrested them at the tower this morning," explained Annette. "Thanks to an anonymous tip." She looked at Terry, whose nod told her what she needed to know.

Terry continued with his story. "Well, the man he and his wife and son had spent Christmas Eve at their cabin. It was down the lane a bit, and their car needed a jump. Luckily they had cables. We were able to get it started without any trouble."

Terry explained that the family had gone away for evening church services Tuesday, but when they came home, they discovered someone had been in their cabin. "He said someone had brought in firewood for them, and had helped themself to a slice of pumpkin pie."

"Oh!" Ruby covered her mouth, her blue eyes wide.

"He showed me a note that they'd left ... thanking them for the pie ... and wishing them a Merry Christmas." Terry smiled over at his sister. "I recognized Ruby's handwriting."

"It *was* me," she affirmed.

"So then, since I knew Ruby and Uncle Will had been nearby, we drove back in further until we got to the last cabin. That's where the station wagon was. The man—whose name is Todd, by the way—helped me dig out the station wagon. We went inside the cabin and got everything out that was yours, found Uncle Will's keys, and Todd drove the car as far as Browns' Store. We figured it would be safe there. Then, after I drove Todd back to his cabin, I took the truck to the Duncans' and walked over here."

"Why didn't you tell Ray and Audrey you'd brought the truck back?" asked Uncle Will.

"I didn't want anyone to see me," said Terry.

"Wow, what a story," breathed Penny.

"Wasn't it kind of hard driving that wagon out of there?" asked Uncle Will. "That snow was pretty darn deep, if I recall."

"Yeah," said Terry. "Luckily, there was a tow chain in the back of the pickup. Todd knew how to attach it, and it was as easy as pie."

"*Pumpkin* pie!" Ruby laughed.

"Your note was the clue," said Penny, smiling at Ruby, who looked so happy on this Christmas night.

"Good job, Ruby." Uncle Will rubbed his niece's head.

It was growing late, so Tim and Penny headed for home after telling everyone good night. Annette took all the empty mugs into the kitchen to soak in the sink. She could hear conversation in the living room, and when she walked back in, her mother was saying, "You can stay longer, Will. You don't have to leave tomorrow."

Uncle Will was on his feet. "My knee is much better, thanks to you, my lady. But I need to get back to Madison. I do have a job ... even though it is only part-time in the winter."

"This is a good time for a talk," said Annette.

Mrs. Vetter made room for Annette next to her on the couch. "Of course. What is it, dear?"

Annette got right to the point. "Mom ... Ruby and Terry both need a home. Social Services in Colorado Springs is making them return there ... unless ..." She looked over at Terry, then at Ruby, then back to her mother. "Unless ... they can stay here — with us."

Mrs. Vetter looked at each of the others, then back at Annette. "What are you asking, Annette?"

"I'd take them," Will interjected, then shrugged. "But Ruby says she'd rather be here."

"Mom, *please* ..." cried Annette.

Terry's face brightened as he looked around him. Ruby came up to Mrs. Vetter and knelt in front of her, then took the woman's hand in hers. "Please, Helen ... please let us be a family together. Terry is both my brother and Annette's brother. I've already told Annette that I want her to be my sister. Will you be our mother?"

Mrs. Vetter was obviously stunned and couldn't speak.

"There will be some legal stuff to go through," said Uncle Will, "but if you ask me, I can't think of a better arrangement."

"Well, I ..." Mrs. Vetter's mouth was wide open as she stared at all their eager faces. There was a long silence in the room, and then she suddenly broke loose with laughter, the likes of which Annette had not heard out of her mother in years. "Okay! Okay! I accept! Ruby ... Terry ... Annette ... I really do think it can work."

Annette, Terry and Ruby all cheered while Uncle Will whooped and started dancing.

"Will, watch that knee!" Mrs. Vetter chided.

"We're gonna be a *family*," cried Ruby.

"Yes, we are!" Annette laughed.

Terry came over and planted a kiss on Mrs. Vetter's cheek, then embraced her. "Helen ... *Mom* ... thank you. I hope I prove to be a worthy son."

Annette jumped up and headed toward the dining room.

"Where are you going?" asked Uncle Will.

"I'm going to call Bob Brennan," she said. "I told him I would. He can tell Sam Chase to help get the paper work started." She looked at the clock. "I don't think it's too late yet to call him."

Uncle Will decided he'd sleep on the living room couch that night. He wanted Terry to have his room back. He planned on driving home to Madison in the morning. After Annette talked to Detective Brennan, she called Penny and told her the great news. By then, everyone was tired and ready for bed.

Later that night, as Annette lay in her bed with Ruby sleeping peacefully next to her, she felt comforted as she gazed out into the hall and saw the light streaming out of Terry's bedroom. She was so glad that her mother was happy again.

Ever since Christmas Eve, Mrs. Vetter's depression had disappeared. There were prospects ahead for so many good times with Terry and Ruby as part of the Vetter family.

Annette had gotten the thing she wanted most for Christmas ... a *boy!* Actually, she thought, she had gotten two boys for Christmas, now that she thought about it—a new brother, and Tim Duncan, a serious boyfriend in the making.

This had been her best Christmas, and to think that all the Christmases that would follow could be just as wonderful.

Just Released ...
The Root Cellar Mystery
by Ann Carol Ulrich

If you like Annette Vetter, you'll also enjoy meeting some of Ann's other characters in this independent novel set in Silver Springs, Iowa.

14-year-old Chris Nesbit is not happy when her family moves away from Milwaukee to a small town in Iowa, where her father is the local paper's new editor.

The first night in their new house, Chris hears a sound and sees the silhouette of a tall man in her room, walking out the door. Too frightened to scream, she waits till morning to tell her parents, but they don't believe her.

Chris is curious about the root cellar in the family's basement, all boarded up and covered with a curtain. She's dying to know what's inside it, but her mother says the cellar is "off limits," even though none of them has even seen it.

Then Chris meets Wendy Young and Wendy's cute older brother Skip, who live across the street. She agrees to join Wendy's club, the P.E.D. (Private Eye Detectives), and together they attempt to solve the mystery surrounding the Nesbits' eccentric next-door neighbor, Mr. North. Not convinced that the strange-looking neighbor deserves to be a suspect, Chris at least will go along with the game.

That is ... until Pamela and Herbert Caldwell enter the picture. These two overly friendly adults from the West Coast are interested in the Nesbits' house for genealogy purposes, yet the girls sense the adults have an ulterior motive.

Meanwhile, night noises continue, and Chris is a nervous wreck. *www.earthstarpublications/RootCellar.html*

About the Author

Ann Carol Ulrich started writing about Annette Vetter when she was 15, growing up in the '60s.

In the Shadow of the Tower is the fifth in the Annette Vetter series.

Ms. Ulrich is a native of Wisconsin, but has lived in Washington, Oregon, Michigan and Ohio. She has spent most of her life in Colorado. She wrote this book while living in Washington state, but intends to write more books about Annette and her friends now that she has returned to her beloved Rocky Mountains in Colorado.

Visit her Author Website at **AnnUlrichMiller.com**, and Annette invites you to check her out on Facebook (*under Annette Vetter, of course*).

The Annette Vetter Adventure Series

The Mystery at Hickory Hill (August 1968) takes place in the Cochetopa Hills of Colorado when Annette and Penny take a vacation out West before school starts.

The Secret of the Green Paint (September 1968) starts on the first day of school, when Annette makes a new friend in her Art class and also notices that new boy who lives on the farm down the road.

The Pouting Pumpkin Mystery (October 1968) celebrates Homecoming at Ravensville High, with a Halloween theme that involves HAM radio.

The Legend of the Lantern (November 1968) takes place over Thanksgiving weekend, during an early blizzard while Annette and Penny baby-sit for the Randt children while their mom has a new baby.

For more information on Annette Vetter books
and others in the Earth Star collection,
visit **www.earthstarpublications.com**

In the Shadow of the Tower
is also available as an eBook at Amazon Kindle

Tim

Penny

Pete

Annette

Terry

Ruby

www.ingramcontent.com/pod-product-compliance
Lightning Source LLC
Chambersburg PA
CBHW070616130626
46556CB00001B/379

* 9 7 8 0 9 4 4 8 5 1 4 2 5 *